The Secret History of

TOM
TRUEHEART

"This charming fantasy . . . is notable for a refreshing lack of violence and dragons—and an abundance of dry wit."
—*Wall Street Journal Weekend Edition*

"Beck's story is a quick read that at once pays homage to its chosen milieu and also serves as a worthy addition to it."
—*Publishers Weekly* (starred review)

"A refreshing and humorous take on traditional fairy tales." —*School Library Journal*

"The bridge between chapter books and novels is as important as the one that takes new readers from picture books to chapter books. It would be difficult to find a better traveling companion for that journey than Tom Trueheart." —*BookPage*

The Secret History of TOM TRUEHEART

Ian Beck

A GREENWILLOW BOOK
HarperTrophy
An Imprint of HarperCollinsPublishers

The Secret History of Tom Trueheart
Copyright © 2006 by Ian Beck
First published in 2006 in Great Britain by Oxford University Press.
First published in 2007 in the United States by Greenwillow Books.

Library of Congress Cataloging-in-Publication Data
Beck, Ian.
The secret history of Tom Trueheart / Ian Beck.
p.   cm.
"Greenwillow Books."
Summary: When young Tom Trueheart's six older brothers all go missing from their adventures in the Land of Stories, he embarks on a perilous mission to save them and to capture the rogue story-writer who wants to do away with the heroes.
ISBN: 978-0-06-115210-8 (trade bdg.)
ISBN: 978-0-06-115211-5 (lib. bdg.)
ISBN: 978-0-06-115212-2 (pbk.)
PZ7.B380768Se 2007 [Fic]—dc22 2006043362

Typography by Sylvie Le Floc'h

First Harper Trophy edition, 2008

Acknowledgments

I should like to thank the following for their reading of early drafts and for their suggestions, encouragement, and help with this book: Liz Cross, Lara Dennis, David Fickling, Hilary Delamere, and Juliet Trewellard, and my family for their patience.

(Dedicated with affection to the memories of Glynn Boyd Harte and Jonathan Gili, beloved friends and collaborators, sadly missed.)

Northern Gate

Eastern Gate

Southern Gate

Part One

The Beginning

CHAPTER 1

Somewhere in the Dark Eastern Woods

Once upon a time, long ago, near the Land of Stories, lived young Tom Trueheart. He was the youngest of the famous Trueheart family of adventurers. He lived far away from here, and even further from now, in a carved and painted wooden house near a busy crossroads, on the edge of a deep dark forest, in the time of fables. He lived with his kindly mother and with his six older brothers.

Tom's six older brothers were all named Jack, after Jack,

their father. Their nicknames were Simple Jack, Jack-a-Napes, Jack the Giant Killer, Jack Sprat, or Jack-a-Dandy.

These Jacks were well known and celebrated throughout the land. Jack, Jacquot, Jacques, Jackie, Jackson, and Jake were very tall, very beefy, very brave, and very noisy young men. On the occasions when they were all at home together, the little wooden house was so noisy, and so crowded with Jacks, that it almost burst at the seams. All of these six brothers were famous for a very good reason.

It was these brave brothers, these same six fabled, heroic Jacks who had carried out all of the toughest, scariest, and most romantic and exciting adventures so far to have happened in the Land of Stories.

All of the great stories had happened to a Jack.

Over the years, the youngest son, Tom Trueheart, had grown into an imaginative, kind, and helpful boy. He was not tall or broad for his age, as all his brothers had been;

he was slight and wiry. His hair was dark and curled naturally, while all his brothers had hair that was straight and worn long like a Viking warrior's.

Tom's hair was hard to tame, and, on the rare occasions when he would let her, his mother had a devil of a time trying to brush it at all. His hair curled around his head in such wild and springy locks that he looked permanently windswept. His eyes were dark, like his mother's, not the clear blue of his father and brothers.

From the earliest age he had suffered from bad dreams after listening to all the scary adventure stories of his older brothers. Dreams of wolves waiting in the darkest parts of the forest with big teeth and dripping jaws. Dreams of ogres and giants and dark dungeons and black-cloaked, smiling villains. Even when there was just Tom and his mother and they had a rare quiet evening on their own together, she would insist that they huddle cozily side by side in the inglenook fireplace (the kind you can actually sit inside), and she couldn't resist telling him one or two of the old and really scary stories. Stories, after all, were the family trade. . . .

There was just one thing: Tom carried in his heart a worrying secret. A secret he kept locked up very tight inside. He was not like his bigger brothers in one other very important way. *He was not at all brave.*

CHAPTER 2

Somewhere Else in the Dark Eastern Woods
The Same Night

Little Jollity Brownfield, an apprentice sprite, flitted through the night forest like a ghost, wrapped in his dark cloak. He moved quietly and fast. His feet crackled and danced over the mounds of frosted leaves. Cousin Cicero had trusted him with his first solo mission, and Jollity certainly didn't want to let him down. He was very nervous about making a mistake. He felt for the bag slung across his shoulder; he could feel the shape of the envelope inside. Phew, he thought, still there, still safe. From somewhere near him a fox barked its unearthly bark, and Jollity nearly jumped out of his skin, it sounded so close. There was a real chill in the air, and it would not be long before the forest would be knee-deep with the first snows of winter.

Jollity soon found the house. It was just as Cicero had described. It was nestled among the trees at the edge of the forest, and close to the crossroads that led to the Four Gates and the roads always taken by adventurers. The house was dark and appeared to be fast asleep, except for a thin ribbon of smoke that drifted from the chimney and the faint light of a night lantern, which hung from the eaves of the little porch and seemed to say, "Welcome, traveler."

Jollity studied the house from the tree line; it was very important that he should on no account be seen. There were three dormer windows along the front and three along the back that overlooked the little fenced-off vegetable plot. There was a smaller attic window in the roof.

"That'll be Tom's room," Jollity said to himself as he skipped across the road and up to the side door. "Very carefully now," he whispered. "Remember your training."

He opened the door, and like a wraith he melted into the dim kitchen. He stood in the shadows and cupped his ear to the inner door. He could hear the faint crackling of a good cozy fire and a deep voice telling an exciting-sounding story (Jacquot back from a recent adventure). He almost tripped over a gaping seven-league boot (the boot of choice for all adventurers) that had been left on the floor just inside the porch. It took him just a moment after that to carry out his first mission. When he was finished, he studied the result from many different positions in the room. He was pleased. He had carried out Cicero's instructions to the letter and as faithfully as he could—mission accomplished.

He heard a sudden shout and a roar of laughter from behind the closed door, which set his little heart beating faster. "That's enough for now, young Jollity," he whispered, and he quietly let himself back out into the cold forest and was soon gone like a shadow through the trees.

On the way up to his bed in his tiny attic bedroom, that night, as on so many other similar nights, Tom's brothers taunted and teased him. They made howling noises as Tom climbed the stairs. They poked their great hairy heads through the gaps in the banisters and stuck their tongues out at him.

"They're only teasing you," his mother said when she hugged him good night. "They mean you no harm. They are wild, and big, and brave, and they're just toughening you up to be the same. And do you know something, Tom Trueheart, you will be the toughest of them all one day, and in your own special way, too. Your turn will come, never fear. Why, you're still far too young to worry about adventuring out in that other big world yet." And she laughed kindly, kissed him on the forehead, and ruffled his hair. When she had shut the door, Tom looked out at the dark forest and the big wide world beyond the garden fence. The trees with their hidden mysteries seemed to press so close to his bedroom window. I'll be twelve in a month, he thought. I can't wait. There was, deep down inside Tom, a secret part that felt ready to tackle an adventure, face a villain, whether animal or human. His mother and his great gaggle of unruly brothers had always treated him teasingly, but fondly, as the youngest of the family. What excited him was the thought that one day he would show them that he could do something daring and brave, too.

CHAPTER 3

The Offices of the Story Bureau

Deeper in among the wintry trees, a long way through the woods from young Tom and his mother and brothers, were the head offices of the fabled Story Bureau. It was an ancient and secret set of buildings. On top of the highest of its sloping gray-shingled roofs was a clock, and on top of that was an iron weathervane in the shape of a witch with her cat riding on her broom.

Near the weathervane was a carved owl. The owl clutched a quill pen in its talons; it presided over the Story Bureau, and the Guild of Stories, as its wise and brooding mascot.

Brother J. Ormestone, a senior story deviser, glanced up at the clock above his desk. He was going to be late for the morning meeting, yet again. He rose at once—like an icy whisper—to his feet. He climbed the spiral staircase, all the way up to the high story conference room. By the time he opened the oak doors, to be greeted by a sea of disapproving faces—his brother scribes, artists, planners, and accountants—he was indeed seriously late.

"I am very sorry, Master," he whispered, and as he spoke the temperature grew noticeably colder. "I was so busy with everything that I'm afraid I lost track of time."

"Well, never mind all that now. I am sure that, as ever, you are most welcome, Brother Ormestone," the Master replied, with a kindly smile.

The morning passed as Ormestone outlined his latest

story plans, which he had polished over the last few weeks.

"If I may, Master," said Brother Ormestone. "I have been completely redrafting the ideas for the story that we discussed at our last meeting, 'The Adventure of the Fair Princess Snow White and the Seventeen Dwarfs.' During the second half of the story, by allowing the young Snow White to escape the hunter and his knife, she can then be found in the woods and sheltered by the seventeen dwarfs. Or *she* could even find *them* in her panic to escape. We will use the northeastern area, the deep woods in the mountains, if our Brother Treasurer could supply a nicely turned-out bright cottage, able to house eighteen, well hidden away, for them all to live in."

"The cottage will not be a problem; there are several we can get ready," said the treasurer, a severe bearded figure in gray, who sat at the other end of the table. "The seventeen dwarfs, now *that* is your problem: I can supply a maximum of seven for any story."

"Seven," said Brother Ormestone in his most chilling

voice. "Seven. Dear me, dear me no. I have worked long and hard on this story, and it definitely involves seventeen dwarfs of varied and, I am afraid, somewhat *twisted* character." He emphasized the word "twisted" in such a way that it caused the Master's skin to crawl, and then Brother Ormestone laughed rather too loudly, which showed his long yellowed teeth.

"Pie in the sky, Brother Ormestone. It would be far too expensive to mount with that number," said the treasurer.

"Too many to draw, anyway. I couldn't fit them all on the page," said a scruffy little Brother Artist who sat next to the treasurer.

"In any case, Ormestone, we have heard enough for now. You have, as usual lately, gone too far in the planning of these stories," said the Master, shaking his head. "There is nothing left for the adventurers to actually do. Your story plans have gotten longer and longer. It is almost as if you are trying to get rid of the adventurers' role altogether. You know the rules as well as the rest of us. We suggest the beginning of things only. We set things up for the adventurers, and they carry out the adventure. It is not up to us to wrap it all up for them and tie a ribbon around it with our name on it."

Brother Ormestone sat down, full of hatred and embarrassment. It was all too familiar a story these days, his gradual and complete humiliation. A mere scribe looked over at him from the other side of the conference table and shook his head in pity. Pity, from a scribe! Brother Ormestone made a loud and sudden crackle as he clenched his bony fingers angrily on his sheaf of loose papers.

"Exactly so," said the treasurer, looking hard at Brother Ormestone, and he simply repeated, "Seven, maximum."

Brother Ormestone dragged himself reluctantly back to his dark, spider-webbed office. He seethed with anger. As usual he had been overruled. As usual those frauds the Truehearts would be sent out on adventures devised by real geniuses like himself. He would finish the stories so much better than they ever could. Truly there was no justice in the Land of Stories. If there were, he himself would be sent out to enact these stories. He would rescue the princess. He would defeat the wolf. He would wear the crown. He had been humiliated once again, and once again the wretched Trueheart family would get the glory. Well, now Julius Ormestone had had enough. He would show them; he would show them all. He had been ridiculed and rejected once too often, and Brother J. Ormestone, story deviser, would soon have his vengeance on the Trueheart family. During the tedium of that story planning meeting, a huge and evil plan had grown, quite suddenly, inside his very twisted, clever, and horribly inventive head.

CHAPTER 4

The Kitchen of the Trueheart House
The First Story Letter, 7:30 A.M.

Breakfast was always a very busy and a very noisy time in the Trueheart household. Great wooden bowls of hot porridge clattered and spilled and slopped, up and down the big table. Tom always helped his mother. He stirred the porridge, and then he dished it out with a big wooden ladle, and then he would clean up, sluicing down the wooden platters and bowls. Meanwhile, his big brothers fought one another over the honey pots, wiped good butter in one another's hair, and threw heels of bread around the place until their mother had to fetch one or the other of them a short, sharp clout on the head.

The main business after breakfast at the start of a new story season was to see whether there had been a delivery. Was an envelope hidden in the house somewhere? If all the brothers were at home together then, sure enough, during the night an envelope would have been silently and mysteriously delivered.

The very morning after Jacquot's return and storytelling, a letter was found. The arrangements of the letter deliveries were a trade secret managed by the sprites. The letters were often tied with gossamer ribbon, which was the finest and most delicate of ribbons, woven by the sprites. The letters would then be hung under a ceiling lamp, or left dangling from a door handle, or some other place. It was Jackson who found the first letter of the season. It was propped just inside the kitchen porch, poking out of the top of a muddy seven-league boot, where young Jollity had left it the night before. Jackson picked it up and brought it over to Jackie. "It's for you," he said.

"Well, everyone," said Jackie with a grin, looking up from his letter. "I'm to be a prince this time; bit of a step up. A promotion from my usual woodcutters, eh, Mother?"

"It's no more than you deserve, Jackie. Here, you take this staff, and you'll need a winter-weight cloak now that the weather's turning." She went and looked out at the dark gray sky above the trees and shivered to herself. The boys' father, Big Jack, had set off in the winter, never to return, and it always worried her when they were starting out on their adventures in the cold weather. She laid a square of the "Trueheart" cotton out on the table and wrapped all the picnic things in it. Her picnics were one of the rituals of an adventure morning. She usually put in a good wedge of hard cheese, some flat crunchy oatcakes, a half loaf of dark pumpernickel bread, a handful of dried fruit, an apple, a cold cooked sausage or two, a small stone jar of ale, and a water bottle. Then she tied the bundle of goodies tightly to the top of a stout packstaff.

Jackie fetched down his sword and scabbard and his battered old travel satchel. He put the letter and some maps in the satchel, and draped his warm winter cloak around his broad shoulders, along with his round shield. The brothers all crowded in the hallway together and wished him well for the adventure. They couldn't resist teasing him, for he had a fondness for princesses.

"Find a nice princess for yourself and try and keep hold of her this time, eh, Jackie," they called out. "It's about time." And they all laughed. Jackie shook his head, but he had a sheepish grin on his face all the same.

"All right then, our mother," Jackie said as he hoisted his packstaff over his shoulder and stepped up to the door. "I'm ready."

Tom pulled the door open for him, and a swirl of cold wind blew all of a sudden into the cozy kitchen.

Tom shivered, and Jackie pulled his cloak tighter about him and ruffled Tom's hair.

"Bye then, young Tom," he said. "Look after our mother. I'll be back in good time for your birthday and with a whole new story for you all to hear."

His mother said, "Now then, Jackie, just you bring yourself back safe and sound. And how about a kiss for your mother?"

Jackie turned and gave her a slightly embarrassed peck on the cheek.

"Make sure you keep warm now," she said, and patted the back of his cloak fondly as he stepped away.

Tom and his mother and brothers crowded onto the porch and watched as Jackie headed for the crossroads. His mother carried on waving long after he rounded the bend, but Jackie didn't look back or wave. He just marched on, his head held high, and as he walked he firmly banged his adventurer's staff up and down on the road.

CHAPTER 5

One by One, They Go Out of the Woods

In the weeks that led up to Tom's twelfth birthday, Cicero and young Jollity took turns at night to visit the little wooden house in the clearing. Young Jollity grew in confidence with every one of his secret letter deliveries, and Story Bureau letters were found for each of the brothers in turn. After Jackie set off proudly to take the role of a prince, it was Jake's turn. His letter was tied with sprite ribbon and hung from one of the oak staffs in the hallway.

"I am to be a prince, too, Mother," he said over his

porridge one morning. "It's the southern gate for me, and a long walk, but to be playing a prince at last, it'll be well worth it."

"Your poor father never got to play a prince," said their mother sadly, and dabbed her eye with the corner of a napkin. The others stared gloomily into their wooden bowls for a moment, until Jack let out a big window-rattling belch, which, as usual, broke the mood.

Other letters were soon found. One was addressed to Jacques, and the next morning there was another addressed to Jacquot, which was hidden inside the big copper saucepan.

Another morning Jack's letter was found outside in the lean-to, tucked into one of the barrel slats of the wooden milk pail. He waved the envelope over his head and stuck his big tongue out at his brother Jackson, who would surely now be the last of the Trueheart brothers to get his letter.

"Now then, Mother and all, let's see what kind of a prince the Story Bureau wants me to be." With a big expectant smile on his face he tore open the envelope, hardly taking time to appreciate the beautifully inscribed name and address.

"Well, well, then, Mother," he said after he had read it, "you'd best be off and make up my adventurer's picnic if you wouldn't mind." He folded the letter and tucked it away into his tunic.

"Hold on," said Jackson. "Not so fast, our Jack; you seem very shy about telling us exactly what kind of a prince they want you to be all of a sudden."

"The Story Bureau thinks so highly of me, they just want me to be . . . myself," said Jack. "I am to play Jack." And he struck a heroic pose, while holding a milk bucket high over his head. "Jack-a-napes, Jack-a-dandy, Jack-i'-the-Green—just good old Jack, in fact. I shall enter Storyland by the western gate; and then we shall see."

Jackson stuck his tongue out at Jack, and Jack threw the remains of the breakfast butter at Jackson's head. Their mother fetched Jack a swift sharp clout around the ear.

"That's for wasting good butter," she said. "Anyway,

stop your baby quarreling and see what I have found in the pantry while you two were showing off good and proper in front of young Tom here. It was sitting on a lettuce leaf between two lumps of my best cheese."

She held a familiar-looking envelope, with familiar-looking script written across it. "*From the Story Bureau,*" it read. "*Strictly Confidential. For the Attention of Mr. Jackson Trueheart, Adventurer.*"

"So you see, here is Jackson's letter after all, and now each and every one of you have your own story assignments, so let there be no more quarreling."

Jackson took the envelope and with a great show of slowness and deliberation he began to open it, cutting the top edge very carefully with his knife. Jackson read his letter, and he took a very long time over it. He appeared to savor it, gulping it down along with his spoonfuls of porridge as he read. Then he looked up with a smile, folded his letter, and tucked it into his belt.

"Well, boo to you, Jack; it seems then that I too shall play the prince."

"Oh yes," said Jack. "How come I get to play a poor simpleton peasant lad all the time, and the rest of you all get to be posh princes, I should like to know?"

"Your turn will come, our Jack," said his mother.

"You look just like a peasant, that's why," said Jackson.

"Oh yes, then pray, exactly what kind of prince will you be, you silly slimy lump?" Jack asked.

"I shall be a *harrumph* prince," said Jackson, and he coughed strangely over one of the words as he spoke it, as if to cover it up.

"Sorry, didn't catch that. What was that?" asked Jack.

"I said I will be a frog prince," said Jackson, going suddenly very whispery and quiet on that same crucial word, and at the same time he blushed bright red for shame.

Jack sensed mischief and his eyes lit up. Tom and their mother looked at each other, puzzled.

"Sorry," said Jack. "We still couldn't catch it, your great highness. It sounded like a 'dog' prince."

"I said, A FROG PRINCE! All right, go on, laugh,

laugh all you like, at least I shall actually get to *be* a prince."

"Oh yes," said Jack, laughing heartily, "a little tiny green one with webbed feet and webbed fingers. No princess for you, then, unless it's the Princess Toad-face, of course."

Their mother put a quick stop to their quarrel with the threat of an ear-boxing for the pair of them. "Riddip, riddip," said Jack, pointing at his brother Jackson with a big grin plastered across his face.

Jack was the first of the two to leave that morning. He set off for the crossroads, still trying to tease his brother Jackson by making the occasional frog noise back at him. The last thing they heard as Jack turned the corner before he was lost to sight was a faint and happy teasing cry of "riddip, riddip."

Jackson himself set off after a hearty lunch. He promised Tom that he would be back in time for his twelfth birthday and with a good present, too. He was dressed from head to foot in green, in readiness for his transformation into a frog. He had a good idea what to expect: he knew that as soon as he entered the gates of the Land of Stories, some sprite or other would some-how do its work, as per the letter, and he would become a transformed and enchanted Frog Prince until such time as the story was properly finished.

"Well," said his mother, dusting her hands down her pinafore front, "that's the last of them off this time, Tom. Now it's just you and me and a quiet cold wait for them all to come back, bursting with their new stories."

"And my birthday presents," said Tom.

"Not forgetting that, of course, Tom. My, my, where does the time go?" she said, ruffling his wild hair.

CHAPTER 6

The Eastern Woods, November 14
The Eve of Thomas Trueheart's Twelfth Birthday, 9 P.M.

The weeks leading up to Tom's birthday had passed in a slow agony for Tom. The house was very quiet and dull without his brothers, but there was one advantage: at least he wasn't being teased all day, and he had plenty of time to dream and play adventures outside with his toy sword and shield. If he wanted to be the best adventurer of them all, he had to practice. Playing and dreaming were important parts of adventure practicing.

Winter was finally settling into the surrounding forest. Frost rimed the deep dark evergreens in the early mornings, and powdered the newly revealed skeletons of the other trees. Magpies chattered harshly together among the branches. Balls of mistletoe hung from the oaks, and all the littlest birds crowded Tom's garden, looking for the last berries and for the scraps of bread and bacon fat that his mother scattered there for them every morning.

In the evenings, after the supper platters and pots were cleaned and put away, Tom and his mother would sit together by a good crackling fire. They imagined what all the brothers were up to and especially how Jackson might be coping with his new life as a frog.

One evening his mother sighed to herself as she looked into the fire, then the wind howled outside and she stood suddenly, pulled the curtain back, and looked out of the window. There was nothing to see but the dark wintry forest beyond the glass.

"I have to say that I'm worried, Tom; I'm very worried indeed. I make a good show of hiding it, but a mother somehow knows when something is seriously wrong. It's not like your brothers to be away for so long.

No story takes this long to complete, and they know how important your twelfth birthday is. They should all be back by now. I really think something terrible might have happened to them."

"They'll be fine, Mum, don't worry. Nothing could happen to them; they're all so brave and strong. They'll be back soon," Tom said as reassuringly as he could, but inside he was worried, too.

They sat together a while longer and watched the logs until they burned out. The embers shifted and fell in on themselves as the fire died. Tom thought about his big brave brothers out there in the world of the cold night, and how perhaps they were lost or in trouble. His mother interrupted his thoughts.

"Bedtime now, our Tom. Come on, upstairs with you. Tomorrow's a big day—your birthday." She went with him, holding a candle to light the way. Tom's shadow was thrown onto the wall and loomed very large above them, as if Tom had grown up all of a sudden as they climbed the stairs.

Tom stopped and said brightly, "I know, they might have all planned to turn up together first thing tomorrow as a birthday surprise."

"They might," said his mother as she tucked him into his deep warm bed. "They might," she said as she blew out the candle, "but don't count on it."

CHAPTER 7

The Story Bureau on the Very Same Night, 10 P.M.

It was in his private rooms at the Story Bureau late in the night, just a little while before Tom's fateful twelfth birthday, that the Master was woken by a fierce drumming and banging on his door.

The Master's inner chamber was a warm, book-lined room situated high up in a tower, perched quaintly on the side of the main building. The Master forced himself out of his warm bed. Something disastrous must have happened to cause such a commotion. He opened his door, which creaked fearfully, as if it, too, was worried about what might be found there.

Standing in front of him, dressed in his characteristic forest green tunic and his camouflage costume of leaves and
twigs and odd patches of forest moss, was an elderly, wise,
and humble wood-sprite called Mr. Cicero Brownfield,
who was busy stamping wet leaves off his boots.

"I am sorry, Master," said Cicero. "I wouldn't have disturbed you like this if it were not a matter of some
urgency."

"Pray, come in," said the Master, "and do shut the door
after you, Cicero, or we'll catch our deaths of cold."

The Master poked at the logs of his quiet fire as the
sprite came in. Then he sat down in his comfortable fireside chair.

"I fear for what you are about to tell me," he said quietly.

"You are right to be afraid, Master," said old Cicero.

"Very well, tell me, then," said the Master, with his
fingers steepled in front of his face. "From the beginning, mind, clearly and carefully."

"We recently delivered the agreed six letters for all the

Trueheart boys. Six big new story starts. They had a letter each, one after the other," said Cicero, "and then they all went off on their new adventures. One letter, one adventure, just as always."

"Of course," said the Master.

"I like to keep an eye on things, Master," said Cicero, "and I have to say I have lately become very worried." He paused and looked directly at the Master. "Not one of them has finished his story yet, not one of those six fine young men has come back."

The Master sat up straight. He looked directly at the sprite.

"None?" he asked.

"Not one, Master," said Cicero and shook his untidy head.

"They should certainly have finished their stories by now."

Cicero continued. "They have all been gone far too long. Something terrible must have happened to them."

"Impossible," said the Master. "It simply never happens."

"Well, I fear it has now," said Cicero sadly. "Adventures

are dangerous things, after all. Think of their father, lost these twelve years, and still no sign; and that's not all. There have been some other reports. Of stories getting so far down the road and then being unfinished. Of characters stuck waiting for things to be resolved. I heard from the southern lands palace that our prince has gone missing, reportedly kidnapped during an expensive ball scene. These things could be expected to happen, a story might stall for some minor reason, but never like this—at least, only once in a blue moon. This is disastrous." And he shook his head.

"Well, the moon looks blue enough tonight, out there in the cold," said the Master. "You were right to come to me, Cicero. What are we to do? The Truehearts are the last of the great adventuring families. Now you say they are all missing, lost in mid-story, and we must send someone to help, but there is no one else to send. The original rules of the Land of Stories are clear." He looked up at the sprite. "Sending help, even if we had anyone we could send, might be seen as infringing on the golden rule of noninterference."

"A debatable point, Master, but as a matter of fact, there is someone we can send," said Mr. Cicero with a quick nod of his head, his face grave and worried under his untidy wreath of leaves.

"I thought you said that all six brothers were missing somewhere in mid-story. They are the last of the line; you are surely not proposing to send out their poor mother on a rescue mission, are you?"

"No, Master, of course not," said Cicero, "but you are forgetting, they are not quite the last of their line. There is another, the seventh brother, the youngest Trueheart, a boy by the name of Tom, who will very shortly," he looked up at the Master's clock, "be exactly twelve years old."

"You mean this bureau will be forced to send a twelve-year-old boy out on a dangerous adventure?"

"It's the only way, I'm afraid," said Cicero. "You should draft a letter for immediate delivery."

"If he is just twelve," said the Master, "then he will be untrained."

"Tom has been watched over, very discreetly, of course, by my young cousin, Jollity Brownfield. He has been keeping an eye on things over at the Trueheart house, and he reports that he has observed young Tom's abilities over the weeks, and he has been most impressed. When I heard the news today, I thought it best to come straight to you. And although young Jollity himself is as yet untested in the field, I would still propose, Master, that we use him to shadow Tom on his mission, to stick to him through thick and thin, whatever happens."

"How is that to be achieved?" the Master asked.

"Through a simple enchantment, a disguise," said Cicero. "Tom won't really be aware that we are watching, and he will certainly not be overtly helped."

"We trusted Ormestone with these six new stories," said the Master, plunging his head into his hands. "He seemed to have reformed lately; we were foolish to trust him. His arrogance could mean the end for all of us. Very well, I will straightaway compose a letter for young

Thomas Trueheart. Inform your cousin Jollity at once of his duties in this matter. My goodness, he will need courage, too. As will all of us."

Wise old Mr. Cicero Brownfield nodded his head in sad agreement.

Brother Ormestone, story deviser, had seemed in those recent weeks to have undergone a very welcome change of character. He had spent all his time in his once dusty, cold, and cobwebbed office working very hard, day and night. By all accounts he had worked well. He had been full of excellent story ideas. He had even tidied and cleaned his little cubicle. His black clothes were no longer covered in dust and bits of dribbled egg yolk. They were now a solid black. His neat boots were polished every morning and shone like mirrors. He had begun to look more like a tall and distinguished bishop than a disheveled and sinister story deviser. His Brother colleagues had commented to one another about his newly discovered energy.

Brother Ormestone spent all his time plotting and arranging. He had created many new story beginnings, new letters, and new clues. He had set off a whole new set of stirring romantic adventures. His letters had been prepared and written up by the best hands and sent out to the adventurer family, the brave Truehearts, one by one. The one unchanging rule, through all past time, was that the adventurer must finish

the story for him or herself, without any help or interference, that he should return and recount the brave
events of the story as they had happened and been
resolved by the adventurer, so that in effect the story
belonged to the adventurer. It was precisely this that
Brother Ormestone had been working so hard, for so
long, and with such astonishing energy to destroy . . .
forever.

CHAPTER 8

Later in the Eastern Woods

He didn't know it yet, but as Tom Trueheart lay asleep deep under the feather quilts of his warm bed, his own personal fate had already been written, sealed, and addressed. Somewhere out among the trees, old and wise Mr. Cicero Brownfield was out again with young cousin Jollity. They had an important delivery to make, the most important delivery that they had ever made. A letter was in Jollity's satchel, a most important letter from the Master of the Story Bureau himself, written in his own hand. The first snow was just settling as they made their silent way through the secret paths of the forest. A fox barked, but this did not trouble young Jollity now.

They reached the little house in the clearing; it looked very cozy and inviting. It sat as quiet as ever, with its smoking chimney, its night lantern, and with just the faint gleam of a candle in one of the upper windows.

"The Trueheart house," said the young sprite, pulling his black cloak closer. He had felt a sudden extra chill.

"Brrr, Jack Frost's working overtime tonight, all right," said Cicero. "Give me the letter and you wait here, Jollity lad. I shan't be but a moment."

The younger sprite stayed in the shadow of the tree line while old Cicero slipped across the road and melted darkly into the house on this most important mission. He was soon back.

"It's time, I'm afraid, lad," Cicero said.

"I know it; I'm ready," said Jollity. "When I looked at the house the last time I was here, I shivered all over, and that goes double now."

"Exactly," said Cicero, "as did I. We sprites have a sixth

sense for these things, you see. This will be an open-ended assignment, and you will be in a state of enchantment for perhaps a long time. You must stay as close to Tom as you can. It means doing all that's necessary, and staying, whatever happens, fully transformed in your enchantment disguise. It won't be easy. You will need to be brave, young Jollity, really brave. We all have faith in you."

They shook hands firmly and said good-bye to each other with a brief hug. Cicero went on his way quickly down the secret paths without looking back. Jollity braced himself for his transformation. He turned and made his way back through the snow to watch over the little house until morning, and to await his special moment, his enchantment.

CHAPTER 9

The First Footprints in the Snow
Tom's Birthday Morning, 6:30 A.M.

It had snowed steadily through the night. Tom was up and dressed very early. He was excited, because at last it really and finally was his twelfth birthday. He was also excited because, as expected, it had snowed. Outside lay the first deep snow of winter. He dressed in his warmest clothes, buckled on his practice sword and leather scabbard, picked up his wooden shield, and crept quietly down to the kitchen. He couldn't see any birthday parcels anywhere. He was hoping for a real blade, an adventurer's sword, as his special present. His mother must still be asleep. He let himself out into a garden that had been transformed by snow. Fresh snow, perfect for . . .

. . . *first footprints.*

At first he just walked around and around. He made lots of deep, crisp prints, and then he took a small hard rubber ball from under his adventurer's tunic. Every morning he practiced catching. He threw the little ball up against the wall of the house or the high part of the fence. He tried to catch it a hundred times in a row without a drop. He had got as far as eighty on his best effort. He would swap hands and try one-hand catching and throwing the ball under his raised leg; he would sometimes make diving catches and try and scoop the ball just before it hit the ground. Good training, his brothers said, for his reflexes.

Then he pulled his wooden sword out from the scabbard on his tunic belt. He held it out in front of him and practiced some strokes with it. He lunged and swiped at imaginary enemy knights or terrifying giants. He had watched his bigger brothers enough times as they trained to know just how such strokes should be made. There was a strict warrior code, and all fights and battles had to be governed by the rules. First he bowed to show respect to his enemy. Then he lined the tip of his sword against the garden fence, where he had drawn some targets. There were faint chalked outlines of knights in armor, hobgoblins, witches, and trolls. He raised the sword again, and lined it against his nose. Then he quietly spoke the family motto, as his brothers always did, "With a True Heart." Then, using both hands, he brought the toy sword down very fast. It made a loud crack, wood on wood, as it hit the fence. The crack repeated in echo across the surrounding forest. It disturbed a flock of birds, who all flew up at once, cawing and squawking in alarm. Then the world went very quiet again.

Tom sheathed the sword and looked up at the dark gray sky. A few flakes of tingling snow were still falling and settling in the branches overhead. Then he noticed that a big black crow was sitting perched on their weathervane. It made a perfect target. He quickly gathered some snow and pressed it together between his hands, making a tight hard snowball. Then suddenly, out of nowhere, as if it had been waiting to get his attention, the crow spoke to him.

Tom stared up at the bird in disbelief. The crow shook itself, fluffed up its feathers, and sat there swaying for a minute. Then it spoke to him again. Tom dropped the snowball. He stared at the bird, and the bird tilted its head on one side and stared back at him.

"What did you say?" Tom asked, astonished.

"Caw, caw," it said, seeming to mock him, staring at him with its beady eyes.

"No, you said something else. There were real words; you spoke to me."

"Caw," said the crow again.

"No, there were proper words. One of them sounded like . . . 'porridge,'" Tom said.

"I said, you'll need *courage*, Tom," repeated the crow

clearly, and it sounded as close as a friendly whisper in Tom's ear.

Then the crow flew up, circled around above the house, and lazily flapped its wings in the cold air. Tom stared up at the bird. He couldn't believe what had just happened. The crow had actually *spoken*, and to *him*, Tom Trueheart. Things like that never happened to him. He had only heard about them in the stories his brothers had told, or in the books he had read. This was his own firsthand experience of . . . well, MAGIC. His twelfth birthday, and something exciting had finally and really happened. He ran back into the house.

"Hey, Mum," he called out, breathless with excitement, "guess what, a crow in the garden just spoke to me, really and truly spoke to me." He ran up the stairs, two steps at a time, and burst straight into her bedroom. "Mum," he said, so breathless and excited now, that his words tumbled over themselves to get out, "there was this big black crow on the roof in the snow, and it said real words to me. It's finally happened, my first little bit of true magic." And then he paused. The little wooden cuckoo clock ticked quietly on the wall. It was a peaceful room and smelled of lavender.

"You're up early," his mother said finally, sitting straight up and rubbing her eyes. "Happy Birthday, Tom," she said with a smile.

"Mum," he said, "a crow spoke to me in the garden, a big black one. Spoke to me, me." Tom pointed at himself.

"Calm down now," she said. "What do you expect; it is your twelfth birthday after all, Tom. That's when things really start to happen to the young men in this family. Goodness, look at all that snow, and no one left to bank the fire up now except your poor old mother."

"I can do that for you now, Mum, don't you worry," said Tom eagerly.

"I know you can, my boy, but it's not the fire I'm worried about," said his mother, shaking her head.

"Still no sign of any of your brothers, I suppose?" she said wearily. "I prayed so hard that they would all be back by now, my poor young Tom. Never mind, we shall try and have a happy birthday breakfast with just the two of us at least." She wrapped herself in her warm dressing gown and together they went down-stairs to the kitchen.

Tom sat down at the big kitchen table. He was surround-ed by empty chairs and empty place settings. They seemed especially empty and forlorn on this morning of all mornings. He hoped he would soon be given his spe-cial birthday present, or at least the little birthday crown, anything to cheer things up a bit.

One by one his brothers had all gone away. Far off on their story adventures being heroes and princes and the like. They had all promised faithfully to come back in time for today. They hadn't come back, though, not one single one of them. Not one of his brothers had kept his promise. This was his most important birthday ever, but they were too busy being princes, no doubt, and living it up; it was so unfair. He bit his lip, suddenly trying very hard to hold back a tear. He had so wanted them all to be there with him. He sat for a moment and listened to his mother humming bravely to herself as she made his breakfast.

He ate his birthday porridge, creamy thick and sweetened with honey. His mother had brought out the little gold cardboard crown she kept especially for birthday breakfasts, and Tom wore that as he ate.

"I fear that something has happened to them, you know, Tom," his mother said. "I'm sure of it now." She went over to the range and made herself a big comforting mug of tea. "They are big enough and brave enough boys, and they're full of courage and cunning, but there are forces out there. . . ." And she shook her head and looked out at the snow, and shivered.

Sorcery was what she meant. It was always a possibility, Tom thought.

It was just then that he noticed the envelope. It was propped up against a big beer tankard on the table right in front of him. Why hadn't he seen it before?

"Look, Mum, a birthday card," he said, and reached across for it. It was a beautiful, big, oblong envelope, made of expensive-looking, heavy, cream parchment.

His mother started to speak. "Tom, I'm afraid it won't be your bir—" She knew with a deadening certainty what this envelope might mean, but Tom interrupted her before she could get the words out.

"Mum," he called out again, "look, it really is for me."

Tom had noticed the neatly formed, thick black writing across the top of the envelope. It read, "*From the Master of the Story Bureau. Private and Very Strictly Confidential.*" Below that in a bolder black handwriting it said, "*For the attention of Thomas Trueheart, Esquire.*"

He read it twice, slowly, to himself. There was no doubt, it said *Thomas*, not *Jack*. The letter was really meant for him, and for him alone.

He held the thick heavy envelope for a moment,

weighing it in his hand. There seemed to be sheets and sheets of paper inside. His mother watched him anxiously, her mouth turned down, and with a look of worry and sadness, even fear, on her face. The envelope might contain terrible news, something they really wouldn't want to know.

Tom's mother turned and looked out the window. She noticed the crow. It had settled in the garden, and she knew straightaway that it must be the one that had just spoken to Tom, by the way it was looking at the house. The big bird was not at all sinister; it looked just as if it was simply watching and waiting, like a good friend of Tom's that had come round to play in the garden.

She raised her hand and gave a little wave to the bird; she felt silly doing it, but somehow felt she must. The bird bobbed its head once, in reply, and she closed her eyes, and took a deep breath. Yes, very well, then, if that is how it must be. She made her mind up and turned back again as Tom finally tore open the envelope and pulled out and unfolded all the sheets of paper from inside.

CHAPTER 10

In Which a New Story Begins, 7:30 A.M.

"*D*ear Tom Trueheart*," Tom read, "*I, as Master of the
Story Bureau, wish you a very happy twelfth birthday. I send
this letter from my personal desk, and in my own hand. The
contents are very private and very strictly confidential. You are
hereby requested to travel at once as an adventurer and enter
the Land of Stories by the Northern Gate. Your mission is to
discover why your brothers, Jacques, Jacquot, Jake, Jackson,
Jackie, and Jack Trueheart have not yet been able to complete
their story missions, and also to discover, if possible, what has
happened to them. There is a suspicion at the bureau that a*

rogue deviser has in some way wished to cause your brothers harm. I write this not to alarm you but to try and explain why the circumstances are so exceptional. Nothing like this has ever happened before.

"In the course of your mission you may be called upon to do dangerous and/or difficult things. You must know that only a member of the Trueheart family may pass through the gates of the Land of Stories on true adventuring business. You will need all the courage of the Truehearts to succeed in your mission. Copies of each of your brothers' letters of direction and instruction are included with this letter. These will at least help you in the general areas and types of stories on which they had so bravely embarked. Enclosed also is a map, a copy of the rules of the Land of Stories itself, and a gate pass, signed by me personally, which will enable you to enter the Land of Stories at any of the entry gates. I wish you a safe adventurous journey and pray for a good story outcome for us all."

Tom unfolded a second sheet of paper. It was the copy of the Rules of the Land of Stories.

THE RULES OF THE LAND OF STORIES
As agreed by the Story Bureau Committee
Witnessed by the hand of the first Master

1. A land of magic and pleasure shall be set up and called "The Land of Stories," which will incorporate Myths, Fables, Legends, Fairy Tales, Nonsense, Rhymes, Poetry, and Adventure. It will be built at the expense of all, for all.

2. The Land of Stories shall occupy the whole of the forested areas and other various lands as shown in the maps attached.

3. The Land of Stories shall be entered through gates at the North, South, East, and West.

4. Adventures shall be carried out only by those born to the adventuring families, and they shall be on true adventuring business.

5. The Story Bureau shall administer, maintain, and furnish the Land of Stories and all its characters, actors, properties, and effects, such as enchanted cottages, beanstalks, castles, trolls, giants, magic flashes, etc., etc.

6. The Adventurers shall be chosen by the Story Bureau.

7. These Adventurers shall carry out the adventures and stories decided on by the Bureau.

8. All the actors and characters within the walls of the Land of Stories shall stay in character and agree to allow the Adventurer to carry out the given adventure/story.

9. The Adventurer shall be allowed to finish the story in his/her own way, without any interference or help.

10. The Adventurer may assume any number of guises

and characters during the story, according to the terms of the original letters of agreement as issued and delivered by the Bureau and/or their associates (sprites, etc.).

11. The story shall be announced by a series of letters and clues open to the interpretation and ingenuity of the individual Adventurer.

12. Secret mechanisms, and sprites and their magic, shall be used when and where necessary.

13. The Adventurer shall return at the end of the adventure and recount his experience to the committee of the Bureau.

14. The Bureau shall then publish, within a reasonable time, the concluded story in book form, available for all to read at a reasonable cost.

15. All decisions of the Adventurer shall be final.

16. Stories must and will flourish, and readers shall love and enjoy them throughout time, in whatever form they may appear.

Tom handed the Master's letter over to his mother. He saw no harm in her knowing the contents; she was a Trueheart, after all. She read the letter and shook her head.

"I knew it," she said. "I felt it so strongly. I knew something was up."

"It can't really be for me, Mum, can it? It doesn't really make sense; it must be a mistake."

"It's no mistake, Tom. The Master of the Story Bureau doesn't ever make mistakes. He means you to go, and go right now, as well. He knows that something terrible may have happened to your brothers. I'm afraid, Tom, I'm really afraid now." She hugged Tom tight and began to cry a little.

Tom pulled away. "I'll go," he said. "I shall find them. I go to the Northern Gate first. It can't be all that hard, can it?" Tom asked fearfully. "Wait, how about this, Mum. Perhaps this letter is all part of a special birthday surprise, a game, a test, a practice story, a little trainee adventure set up by the Master of the Story Bureau, and maybe by my brothers as well, see. It's the first stage of my training, of becoming a real adventurer. They will finally see what a brave and resourceful boy I can be."

"I only wish that could turn out to be true," said his mother. "But, sadly, I think the letter is real and not a game."

"They'll be just down the road, a short walk north in the fresh snow. It could be fun," he said, keeping a brave smile on his face.

"We must all rely on you now, Tom," his mother said quietly. "I know it doesn't seem fair, seeing as it's your birthday, and you're only just twelve and all, but you are a Trueheart, young man, through and through, and Truehearts don't give up, do they, my Tommy?"

"No, Mum, they don't. Right, then, I will go, and go right now. Come on, I'll show them."

His mother slowly fetched all the things the brave adventurer might need. She brought out one of the oak pack-staffs—a shorter lightweight one, more suitable for a boy of Tom's build. Then she found the last unused square of the special "Trueheart pattern" cotton in the dresser drawer. She laid it out flat on the table. She had to hold back a tear, for she had been saving this last little square of cloth for when Tom was finally trained and ready for his first proper story. She had never thought in her wildest dreams that she would be making up his first adventure picnic so soon, and under such circumstances. She straightened, took a deep breath and fetched the pumpernickel bread, some cheese, a cooked sausage, some dried fruit and nuts, and an apple. She put some candle stubs and matches in. She automatically pulled out a stone bottle of strong ale from the larder, but then she looked across at Tom, who stood with his back to her for a moment, looking out of the window at the snow. She noticed how young and vulnerable he looked with his narrow shoulders and his silly wild hair, so she put the ale back. She found something more suitable tucked away on a back shelf of the larder, a bottle of her home-brewed ginger beer, and she added that to the picnic instead.

She wrapped the food and drink in the Trueheart cloth and tied it good and tight to the little staff. Tom went and found his best pair of stout boots; they were not quite "seven-league," but they would be good enough. He grabbed a shield from the rack, buttoned up his warm tunic, and he was ready. He stood for a moment in the quiet kitchen.

"I'm twelve years old now, Mum. I'll be all right, really, I promise," he said. "I'll find out what happened. I'll show them all, I'll show everyone I can do it, just you wait. I'll bring them all back safe and sound, Mum, I really will."

The thought of setting off alone, beyond the safety of his garden gate and out into the unknown world, a world of cunning wolves, and sprites, and danger, and transformations, and real adventure, still scared him. His only adventures so far had all happened inside his own mind, in the sheltered safety of his own garden. His battles had only been with imaginary enemies and monsters, and using just a toy sword. There was, however, that deep-down part of him that felt ready, felt strong. Somewhere inside him was an as-yet-untapped well of Trueheart courage.

"Keep that map and all the letters with you, son, and watch out for other letters and clues as they come," his mother said. "That's how it always works, Tom; you'll find out as you go along."

He was to enter by the Northern Gate. It led to the mountains, which would be covered in snow and ice, and to polar bears, trolls, and dwarfs, and whiskered hobgoblins. He picked up his packstaff and went to the door and opened it. Outside, the world was very quiet, and strangely bright with all the light reflected from the crisp snow. He stepped out onto the porch.

"You keep warm now, Tom, and be very careful," his mother said.

"I will, Mum."

"And when you find those brothers of yours, you make sure you give them a really good telling-off for missing your birthday," she said with a sniff.

"I will, Mum, I promise. See you soon."

"Come on now, you can at least spare a kiss for your mum."

Tom went back and gave his mother a hug. She kissed him on top of his wild, curly head.

"Don't worry, Mum, see you soon. I'll be back in two shakes of a lamb's tail," he said. He turned, walked up to the gate and hesitated, with his hand on the cold iron latch. Something was worrying at him. Something someone had said to him very recently. The thought of what they had said had crept up on him from the back of his mind and now made everything seem suddenly darker, and much more dangerous. What was it? Oh yes, that was it.

The crow; it had spoken to him all right, but what had it actually said? The crow had given him a warning, an omen, it was called. He hadn't thought about the words themselves in all the shock and excitement. He looked around the garden and on the roof for the big black bird, but it had flown away.

"You'll need *courage*," is what the crow had said, *courage*. That meant he would really have to face danger and trouble, and he was frightened of danger, and he was frightened of trouble. But they seemed to have come calling anyway, both for him and his brothers. He had no choice now; it was clear what he had to do, he just wished he didn't have to do it all on his own.

You'll need courage.

He turned and gave his mother a final brave smile and a wave, took a deep breath, and then opened the garden gate and stepped out.

His mother watched him walk away slowly through the deep snow. After all, she thought, every big adventure starts with that one little step. Before she shut the door she watched Tom walk as far as the bend. She looked at the empty road after he had gone and waited a moment in the quiet of the cold morning.

"Shake, shake," she said, and shook her hand twice, as if it were a lamb's tail, but although she waited a moment longer, Tom didn't come back.

Part Two

The Middle

CHAPTER 11

Tom Sets Out on the Road North
The Forest, 9 A.M.

When Tom was finally out and on the road, everything loomed very large, and distinct, and seemed to be so
much bigger than he was. The dark forest pressed in toward
him from either side of the road, and he felt suddenly as if
he had been shrunk by sprites to the size of a tiny dor-
mouse. He was out alone in a big, big world where the
trees seemed very much taller and very much darker than
they ever did from the safety of his garden. There were
strange noises to worry about as well. The trees themselves
creaked and moaned eerily as they shifted together in

the wind. On the ground, twigs cracked and snapped as unseen creatures tracked past him through the undergrowth. The rooks cawed and shrieked and shouted to one another in the treetops. Tom had to brace himself; he imagined what one of the Jacks might say to him if this was a training session—which of course some tiny hopeful part of him still believed it was.

"Come on," they would have said, "it's daylight, and you're not that far from home. You can do this. It's your birthday; you're twelve years old now, and practically grown up. Get on with it."

Tom tightened his grip on the packstaff and carried on. He planted his feet down very firmly, one after the other, left right, left right. He made as deep a set of bootprints in the snow, and with as much noise, as he could manage. He hoped that would scare off any wolves or predators, and in any case it helped to make him feel a lot warmer and a lot better. By the time he reached the crossroads he was making good time, and there sat the talking crow, large as life, on the north point of the sign.

"There you are, Mr. Crow," Tom said, as brightly as he could. "I thought you'd flown away somewhere."

The crow shifted its balance, tilted its head on one side, and studied him for a moment. It did not reply at first.

Tom looked up the long straight road that led north through the forest. That was where his first adventure was taking him. His destiny lay down a long road, through the middle of a forest toward an unknown place. The crow turned its head and said, "You can call me Jollity, by the way," and then took off suddenly and flew straight on ahead as if to say, "Come on, this is the way." Tom thought that it was an odd name indeed for a crow, but then Tom might seem an odd name for a person, to a crow. He had no choice, really, but to set off and follow it.

CHAPTER 12

The Northern Gate

The crow flew on for a while and then stopped and seemed to wait for Tom. As soon as Tom had nearly caught up with Jollity the crow, the bird took off again, and so the morning passed. Tom walked, and the crow flew on, a little way ahead of him; it was like a game of catch-up. They were surrounded by the seemingly endless dense fir trees of the forest, with the long straight road cutting right ahead through the middle of the trees. There were no other travelers.

After hours and hours of steady walking, Tom saw

quite suddenly a wide looming shadow ahead on the road. Then a league or so farther on, the trees thinned out. The deep forest ended in a very straight line, and Tom stepped in one short stride from the middle of trees and forest into a bright patch of road where the snow was all piled up against a long wall. The wall stretched all the way from one horizon to the other. There in front of him, stretching across the road, was the Northern Gate of the Land of Stories.

The gate took the form of a stone arch supported by tall pillars. The bases of the pillars were formed of big cubes of stone, chopped and roughened and pitted, so that they looked all weathered and ancient. The stones were cut into a curved arch and on the keystone was carved the head of a polar bear, which glowered down at the roadway. Sitting huddled in a little patch of sunshine near the central barrier (a red-and-white striped pole) was the gatekeeper. Tom approached and the man looked up from his newspaper.

"Yes?" said the gatekeeper.

"We are here on adventuring business. May we pass, please?" said Tom.

"Do you know how many annoying kids like yourself come up here every day and try to sneak past me?" said the gatekeeper.

"No," said Tom.

"Well, neither do I." The gatekeeper sniffed, looking Tom up and down, and then he looked over at the crow, which looked straight back at him with its bright eyes. "But there have been some," he added.

"We are here on important business," said Tom.

"Yes, and I'll be a monkey's uncle," said the gatekeeper.

"That could easily be arranged," said the crow, lifting its wing. "Show him the pass, Tom." Tom opened his satchel and found the pass card signed by the Master.

The gatekeeper looked at Tom, and then at the crow. Then the gatekeeper looked down at the pass in his hand.

"You should have said you were a Trueheart, young man," the gatekeeper said, now plainly a little nervous.

"You didn't give me a chance," said Tom.

"I'm sure I let one of your brothers in through this gate a while ago," said the gatekeeper.

"That's why I'm here," said Tom. "I'm looking for my brothers."

"He went off about his business, a real prince among men," said the gatekeeper. "I've not seen him since, mind."

With that, the gatekeeper lifted the red-and-white striped barrier, and Tom and Jollity the crow stepped through the wild Northern Gate into the Land of Stories.

Tom walked for a little while along the road. He held his packstaff jauntily over one shoulder, and as he walked he imagined how many times his brothers or even his father might have walked this same road. The surrounding landscape didn't seem so very different from before, once he left the gate and the wall behind. The trees were perhaps in better trim. They looked somehow even more dramatic than before, as if different species of tree had been deliberately grown beside one another for maximum impact. Tom was alert now for anything. He had entered a magic walled secret world where he knew almost anything was possible. He would need his wits about him now.

The crow flew on ahead of Tom, stopping to rest every now and then as he had before, seeming to test things, as it were, keeping an eye open perhaps for any trouble ahead (which, of course, is just what he was doing), and then allowing Tom to catch up with him, and flying ahead a little way again. And so they went on until Tom realized just how hungry he was. So he sat down by the road and opened up his bundle. Among the picnic treats he found a note that his mother must have sneaked in when he wasn't looking.

"I will be thinking of you, Tom. Be brave, keep warm, keep safe, and hurry back with all those big bad brothers of yours. Love, Mum. XXXX"

Tom pulled out the stone bottle of ginger beer. "Cheers. Thanks, Mum, and Happy Birthday to me," Tom said, and he raised the bottle just as his brothers would raise their tankards of ale before a good story, and as he drank his ginger beer, he was reminded of home and his mum and felt a sudden twinge of loss.

"Never mind," he said out loud to no one in particular, trying to cheer himself up. "I'm sure I'll be seeing them all again soon."

"Of course you will," the crow replied.

"You haven't said much so far, have you?" said Tom.

"I like to speak when I have something interesting to say," said Jollity the crow.

So they sat near each other for a while and Tom enjoyed his picnic. He offered some of his scraps to the crow, who seemed to take great pleasure in them.

After lunch Tom and the crow carried on with their journey. They eventually came to a crossroads. The crow flew up and landed on the point at the top of the signpost. The four hands pointed down another four possible roads. Some sprite ribbon was looped around an envelope that hung from the sign pointing west. The sign was too high for Tom to reach even with his staff, so the crow flew up, inched along the post, and busied itself undoing the filmy green sprite ribbon. Eventually the envelope fluttered to the ground at Tom's feet.

It was addressed to *Thomas Trueheart, Esquire.* He opened the envelope and slowly unfolded the parchment letter. It was written in the same handwriting as the first letter. This time the message read,

> *Dear Tom,*
> *Be very, very careful. You should now travel west to the village of Snoreing. Stay at the Briar Inn for news of your brother Jackie. Courage, young Thomas, courage.*
> *The Master*

"What does it say?" asked the crow.

"It says we must travel west, to a village called Snoreing, whatever that means, funny name for a place."

"Is it?" said the crow. "I thought it was what sleeping people sometimes did?"

"What?" said Tom.

"Snore, of course. You know, snoring: haaarnk, wheee haaarnk wheee," said the crow noisily.

"Oh, *snoring*," said Tom. "Yes, of course, big Jacques used to snore all the time." And he smiled as he remembered the night when his brothers threw all their pillows and bolsters across the bedroom at Jaques to make him stop his terrible snoring noises. Tom was getting used to Jollity the talking crow. He had to admit to himself that it was very nice to have someone to talk to and be on the road with.

"Well, it certainly means us to go west, which is that way," said the crow, pointing with its wing down the road to one side of them.

"I know, I know," said Tom.

"Only testing," said the crow.

So the two friends set off together down the long road to the west.

CHAPTER 13

The Sleeper in the Castle
Somewhere in the Western Lands
Some Time Before

Tom's older brother Jackie had been the first to leave the house in the woods to set off on a new story adventure. Once he was through the chosen gate he had walked for a whole day and night through snow and wind, well wrapped in his winter-weight cloak. Then suddenly the snow and the trees just ran out, the deep forest simply ended in a very straight line, and Jackie stepped in one short stride from the middle of deepest winter into a bright sunlit world of spring. On a signboard at the side of the road, picked out in gold

letters, were the words WELCOME TO THE WESTERN
LAND OF STORIES.

Jackie was as far west now as he had ever been. The
people seemed a jolly enough crowd. They waved and
smiled at him when he passed them on the sunlit road.
He supposed they were glad to see an adventurer prince
busy on an exciting adventure among them.

He found the village of Snoreing as his letter had suggested, and sure enough there was the inn with the painted sign of the Briar Rose. He ordered a room and supper from the landlord and settled in for the evening. "Always good to welcome an adventurer like yourself," the landlord said. "You'll be off to the castle in the morning, I'll be bound."

"Castle?" Jackie asked.

"You can't miss it, 'tis all covered over, top to bottom, with thick briars and twisty old roses, with those gert sharp spikes. The thorns are as big as your arm, impossible to get through. Others have tried," the landlord said.

"Thorns?" Jackie asked.

"'Tis all overgrown since the spell; well, so they say," said the landlord, warming to his theme.

"Spell?" Jackie asked.

"There's a sleeping princess needs rescuing. Whole place is asleep, but you can't get in, what with the briars and thorns all over it, see. Now there's a job for an adventurer like yourself and no mistake."

There was a mist across the land the next morning as Jackie, in the guise of a good, brave prince, set off after a fine breakfast. He had enjoyed the landlord's fresh eggs, bacon, mushrooms, and even a slice of homely fried bread, all washed down with good strong tea.

He had left his winter cloak with the landlord, and set off on the road to find the castle and effect the brave rescue. His bundle was nicely full of fresh provisions and a canteen of ale. He walked the twisty road for a while, wary of the blurred and foggy surroundings. He banged his staff down hard on the road as he walked. That should keep any cutpurses away, he thought. He kept a sharp lookout for an Enchanted Castle.

He could smell it before he could see it. There was a sudden sweet perfume on the air. It was the overpowering scent of millions of roses. Jackie turned a bend in the road, and there up on a hill was the towering blurred outline of a castle. It was just as the landlord had described it.

The castle was completely covered over with briar stems and roses. Jackie could just make out the shapes of the huge thorns and the densely twisted branches. Leaves, thorns, and stems were jumbled together all around and knotted in a mighty tangle. He drew his sword and walked up the path.

There was a deep silence over the whole area, with not even the sound of birdsong. There was just the drip, drip of water as the mist collected and fell in runnels among the briar leaves. He could see no way in. So, Prince Jackie, true to the family spirit of action and "derring-do," decided to waste no time. He must go in and somehow find and rescue this lovely princess.

He straightaway began hacking at the twisted briars and thorns. He had to keep his shield close to his sword arm to protect himself from all the vicious spikes. After an hour or so of very hard work he had cut a low tunnel through the thorns and twisted stems. The tunnel led all the way over the drawbridge and up to the castle gate. He worked for a while on the little door in the middle of the gate until finally he managed to force it open. He stepped in through the door, only to be met by the tall figure of a thin man in black clothes with a full head of sleek white hair.

"Good morning, Prince Jackie," said the man, and he produced a large white pocket handkerchief, and with a great flourish held it out toward Jackie. There was a strong sweetish perfume on the cloth. Jackie was so taken aback, so confused by the sudden appearance of this sinister figure, that he simply leaned forward out of sheer politeness and sniffed at the cloth. The smell was very sweet, stronger even than the overpowering scent of the roses. For Prince Jackie the world suddenly began to swim and dissolve all around him, and he found himself falling, falling, all the way down to the soft and welcoming ground.

CHAPTER 14

The Western Lands
Some Time Later

Tom and the crow traveled west as the sky darkened. The landscape around them had changed again. From the northern firs and snows beyond the gate, they had followed the map as best they could and finally traveled into another forest. This was not like the pine and fir forest of before. Here were oak and beech trees, rounded little hills, and streams. There was a warm wind, and strong golden late sunlight, and it was thirsty work just walking. Tom had to refill his empty stone ginger beer bottle often, as well as his water canteen, from one of the rushing roadside streams. Once, as Tom drank, Jollity the crow settled for the first time on his shoulder. Tom felt suddenly proud that the crow should trust him enough to sit on him, and they walked on for a while, with the crow bobbing happily up and down on Tom's shoulder.

"Crows get tired, too," said the crow after a while. "It's getting dark, Tom. I think we should rest up for the night. You've walked a long way and you couldn't get all the way back home now even if you tried. We've come many, many leagues, I should think."

Home seemed a very distant place now, somewhere far back among all those dark trees. An owl hooted from somewhere in the woods and Tom felt a little twinge of panic, of fear. Where would they spend the night? He was tired now himself. He yawned and stretched his arms out so that the crow flew suddenly up in the air with a surprised squawk.

"Goodness me, I was falling asleep, too," said the

crow. "We must find somewhere to rest right now. Come on."

Tom settled himself under a canopy of leaves and welcoming branches. He rested his head on the travel satchel, said good night to the crow, and was, surprisingly, soon asleep. Must be all that walking, he thought to himself as he drifted off.

The crow flew around the woods while Tom slept and eventually found the hooting owl sitting on its home branch deep among the trees. He gave a secret and urgent message to the owl, then flew back and settled himself to sleep on one of the branches overlooking Tom.

The owl passed on the message to another owl, who passed it to another and so on all the way down the line, until by the next morning, when old Mr. Cicero Brownfield was out in the eastern forest, the message finally reached him. "Tom is safe and watched and in the west," was the gist of it, with a few bird elaborations about wind speed, night hunting, and so forth. Cicero reported the news to the Master over a nice cup of fresh acorn coffee.

"So far, so good," said the Master, "but let's keep our ears to the ground, Mr. Cicero, just for safety's sake."

CHAPTER 15

The Western Lands, 7:32 A.M.

Tom and the crow made a strange breakfast of nuts and water, then they went back to the main road and continued to walk westward as Tom's shadow stretched along the road in front of them. They soon reached a road sign that pointed in the direction of Snoreing, some five leagues distant.

"Look," said Tom. "That's the way."

When they reached the village Tom saw that it was a sleepy little place, with just a few thatched houses built around a green, a duck pond, and an inn. Some happy ducks swam on the pond, but there was no one about in the little high street. The old inn was called the Briar Rose, and a man was outside sweeping his doorstep. The crow flew off, settled near the pond, and chatted to the ducks while Tom approached the landlord of the Briar Rose.

"Good morning, sir," said Tom.

"Morning, young fellow," said the landlord, resting his broom for a moment against the porch and brushing his hands on his apron.

"I wonder if you could help me? I am looking for a traveler who might have stayed here recently," Tom asked politely.

"Lots of travelers pass through here, my good lad," said the landlord.

"This would be a very tall young man, with broad shoulders. He might have had a circular shield and a sword like this." He gestured to his own sword and scabbard, which were tucked under his cloak.

"Plenty like that; they have armor, helmets, shields, swords, you name it. We get all sorts through here, it's that sort of place," said the landlord, stroking his chin thoughtfully.

"His name was Jackie," said Tom.

"Jackie, Tommy, Dickie, Harry, we get them all here on account of . . ." The landlord suddenly stared at Tom's packstaff. "Tell a lie," he said, "there was someone here called Jackie. He carried a bundle wrapped in that very same cloth. With that same pattern on it, those hearts." He pointed at Tom's staff and bundle. "Big young lad he was, broad shouldered, a proper nice adventurer. A real prince, and very generous with his ale in the snug bar, as well."

"Where did he go?" Tom asked.

"He went off to the enchanted castle. He left very early quite some days ago, but he still took the time to enjoy one of my wife's fine breakfasts." The landlord nodded his head and smiled. "Ah yes, a real royal gentleman. Very pleased with that breakfast he was, too. He never came back, mind. He left his cloak and all, but we haven't seen him since."

"Please, sir, could I see his cloak? He was one of my older brothers, you see, and I am on an adventure mission, a quest to find them."

"I don't know," said the landlord, thinking for a moment. "Mind you, you seem a nice enough lad, and you *are* sporting the selfsame bundle cloth as that prince. You'd best come along with me, then."

The landlord ushered Tom into the inn. It was dark inside the bar as the shutters were still closed over the windows.

"You wait here," said the landlord.

The crow scampered in through the open door and sat on Tom's shoulder.

"Jackie was here," Tom whispered. "Traveling as a prince. He went off to an enchanted castle."

"Enchanted," said the crow; then the landlord came back with Jackie's cloak, and the crow shut up quickly.

"Friend of yours?" said the landlord.

"Yes, he's very tame," said Tom. "I raised him from an egg."

"Well, well," said the landlord. "The things you see in

this game, nothing whatever surprises you after a while. Here's the cloak, then."

It was Jackie's all right.

"Nice wolf fur collar," the landlord said, peering over Tom's shoulder.

"I'll take this with me, if I may, sir. Now, you said something about an enchanted castle?"

CHAPTER 16

Still in the Western Lands
The Enchanted Castle

Tom and the crow found the enchanted castle easily enough. As they stood looking up at it, Tom thought what a very strange sight it was. The huge castle rose high into the clear sky and was covered all over with leaves and roses and thick thorny branches. There was a deadly hush of quiet over everything, as if time itself had stopped. They went up to the base of the building where all the growth began, and Tom walked all the way around the edge, looking up at the towers and pinnacles shrouded with prickly greenery. The crow flew up high among the leaves, but could see no sign of life anywhere at all.

"Everything," he told Tom, "seems to be asleep."

Tom noticed there was a low tunnel, which looked as if it had been recently cut through the tangle of briars. Jackie, he thought. There was no sign of Jackie now; he had disappeared, either into the mystery of the enchanted castle or else into nothingness. The crow stayed behind at the entrance, while Tom bent low into the tunnel and worked his way along, easing carefully past the jagged rows of sharp thorns.

After a while he crossed the wooden slats of the draw-bridge and came to a little wooden door set into the middle of a much larger and wholly overgrown door. The little door stood half open, and behind it was a deep, deep darkness. Tom took a breath and eased himself through the gap into the shadows beyond. Some way in front of him, he was aware of something pale, a shape hovering in the blackness. He was gripped with a sudden fear. He could hear a strange noise, too, a soft animal rumbling sound, which came from the deep dark space in front of him. Tom could do nothing. He was rooted to the spot in terror. He could neither go forward nor back. He was paralyzed, his ears seeming to magnify every sound intensely. He could hear the water that dripped off the briars and leaves. He could hear the breathing of the fierce animal somewhere in front of him. It was the low steady rhythm of a hungry wolf, which Tom imagined was waiting for him. He took a step back and felt something sharp—the point of a dagger held by a silent cutpurse perhaps? He stood still with the thief's sharp dagger pressing into his back, and the fierce animal waiting in the dark ahead. Of the two evils he thought that perhaps he could at least trick a cunning wolf and escape. His brothers certainly would have. He stepped forward. He had been so long in the tunnel that his eyes had become accustomed to the gloom, and as he moved beyond the doorway and into the dim courtyard beyond, he saw the pale shape more clearly.

It was no wolf; it was a man lying on the ground all tangled up in leaves and roses. What he had heard were the man's snores as he slept in the thicket. Tom went over to look at him. It was a soldier, dozing among the flowers. He had a spear and a royal banner draped across him and he opened one eye as Tom looked at him. Tom stepped back.

"She's upstairs, top of the tower," the soldier whispered with a wink.

"Who's upstairs?" Tom asked.

"The princess, of course. You've done well, my lad, to get this far; others have tried and failed," said the soldier, sitting up a little and shaking his head. "Once you get through the tower door the roses stop. They are mainly out at the front for show; took them ages to do. Just get the rescue over with so we can all wake up, only don't tell anyone I told you. You haven't seen me, if anyone asks. I was fast asleep," he whispered.

"We're all asleep," came another voice from deeper inside the bush.

"I see," said Tom. "I don't think I'm meant to rescue anyone; it's not my job, you see. I'm looking for one of my brothers: tall, fair-haired, beefy, answers to the name Jackie or Prince Jackie?"

"Could be anyone," said the soldier very quietly and very grumpily.

Tom said good-bye to the snoozing guard and went across the courtyard to the tower door.

Once inside it was gloomy because the windows were all overgrown, but the twisty stairs were clear and he was soon able to climb right to the top. There were some pale, blush pink roses draped around the door. The effect was romantic rather than threatening. Tom pushed through them, opened the door, and stepped in. There was a bed hung with curtains in the middle of the room. It was raised on a platform and the curtains were decorated with a pattern of roses and flying cupids loosing their little arrows. Tom stepped up to the bed, mounted the platform, pulled the curtains apart very slightly, and peeped in. He still feared a wolf or worse might leap out at him, but when he looked down he saw that a young woman lay asleep on top of the covers. She had fair hair and pale skin. Her lips were crimson and her dress was green and patterned over with leaves. She looked like a rose herself as she lay there so fast asleep.

"At last," came a sweet voice from somewhere.

Tom backed out of the curtains and looked around the room. There was nobody else there. He put his head back through the curtain opening. The girl had one eye open now. She shut it quickly.

"Do something, then," she whispered out of the side of her pretty mouth. She opened her eye again. "Oh no," she said, "you're a bit young, aren't you? Is this the best they can do?"

"It was meant to be my brother, I think this is his story. I'm really looking for him—he's taller, older, better looking—you'd like him if he was here, and here is where the clues have led me."

"Look, I'm sure you're a very nice boy and all that," the princess whispered very quietly, "but I have a terrible curse on me: to sleep for a hundred years. That's a long time to lie here wondering. I need rescuing by love's first kiss now before it turns into two hundred, all right?"

"Don't worry, miss, when I find him I'll send him straightaway," said Tom suddenly standing to attention. "I am Thomas Trueheart of the adventuring Truehearts, you can rely on me, miss . . . erm . . . sorry, Your Highness."

"Lean a little closer," said the princess. "You're sweet," she said, and gave him a little peck on the cheek, "but how am I going to get back to sleep now, I feel so wide awake?"

After he stopped blushing, Tom thought for a moment and said, "My mum always sang me a lullaby when I couldn't get to sleep."

"Good idea," whispered the princess, "try it."

"What me, sing?"

"Please, please, pretty please."

So Tom sang a lullaby, the only one he could remember. It was "Hush-a-bye, Baby, on the Treetop," which, if he thought about the words, was more likely to wake you up in terror than send you off to sleep. It seemed to work, though. His voice echoed around the stone walls, and within a few moments the princess appeared to be fast asleep again.

"I'm off to find my brother now," Tom whispered, "and as soon as I find him I'll send him straight here to rescue you, I promise." There was no reply; the lovely princess was back deep in her enchanted sleep.

Tom set off at a lick back down the tower stairs. He said good-bye to the sleeping soldiers and turned and went out of the overgrown doorway. He crept back down the dangerous, thorny, spiky tunnel and back out into the open air. He saw the crow perched on a bush of roses.

"We must find Jackie," said Tom. "He's really needed here to finish this story before it's too late."

The crow flew down and sat on Tom's shoulder. He had an envelope in his beak from the Story Bureau. "It arrived Special Delivery via various birds," he said. Tom opened the envelope and read the letter out loud.

Dear Tom Trueheart,
I understand that you are making progress and are safe
so far. I must warn you of the malicious and clever man
who, it appears, seeks the destruction of the Trueheart

family. You must be vigilant and very, very careful in your travels. He is a tall lean man with white hair and he wears black clothes. The stories he devised were, as far as we know, scattered across the whole of the Land of Stories.

If you have arrived in the west then your next direction, after you have followed up any clues, should be due south. Enjoy the sunshine.

Kind regards,

The Master

"Well then, Crow, it looks like we are to travel south."

"I'll be right ahead of you," said the crow.

So it was that Tom and the crow set off on their next journey, to the south.

CHAPTER 17

Jake's Story
Some Weeks Before, the Southern Lands
Sunny, very little wind, an even warm temperature, 2:33 P.M.

Jake's adventure took him through the warm, welcoming Southern gate. He found himself by the second day walking through a very neat and tidy landscape. It consisted of little soft, green, and very rounded hills that looked as if they were made of squishy marshmallow. As Jake walked, he noticed that nearly all the trees he was now passing had been cut into shapes. Sometimes they were severe, such as pyramids and cubes and spirals, and sometimes they were silly and fanciful, such as peacocks and bears and teacups. It was as if the whole of the surrounding landscape had been brushed, and trimmed, and swept, and painted, and manicured.

The houses Jake passed on his travels all seemed very rarefied, too. Palaces were scattered here and there, and were even grander than the houses. Strange place for an adventure, he thought. Why, I've only got to run a little bit too hard, or stretch my arms out a little bit too wide and I could end up breaking a house down or messing up a whole garden full of these spindly looking trees, and he shook his head. He did wonder sometimes at the sprites and story devisers and the wicked little games they liked to play. Just to be sure, he checked the Story Bureau letter in his travel satchel. There it was, in the familiar black ink of the bureau scribes.

Dear Adventurer,

You should aim to arrive at the Royal Palace in the late afternoon, where you will be expected and will be known as Prince Charming. At the palace you will be given appropriate clothing for a grand prince and your other duties will then be made known to you.

Yours sincerely, etc.

"Must be the place, then, all right," he said to himself and carried on down the road.

The Grand Royal Palace, 4:59 P.M.

Jake marched straight up to the front door of the huge royal palace. He was indeed expected and was led at once to a fine chamber. Fresh clothes, fit for such a charming prince, were laid out on an enormous four-poster bed. A very thin man with white hair and dressed in black clothes showed him everything, exclaiming as he did so with great solemnity and with a sinister glint in his eye.

"Look at this velvet and ermine," he hissed, "this silk and satin. So lovely and fitting for such a prince, my liege." Jake was obliged to rummage through all of the offered clothes and choose an outfit.

"Sire," the servant said, bowing low, "it is felt that a ball should be held to celebrate our Prince Charming's birthday, and to that end I have drafted this invitation." He handed a roll of parchment to the prince. As Jake took it from the servant their fingers touched for an instant, and Jake felt a strange all-over chill envelop him.

His Majesty the King and Her Royal Highness the Queen
invite you to a masked ball
to celebrate the Birthday of the noble
Prince Charming
at the Royal Palace
Food and Fireworks
Carriages long after midnight

"Very well," said Jake. "That seems clear enough."

The sinister servant appeared delighted. He whisked the parchment away to arrange for its immediate distribution. All Jake really wanted to do was have a proper adventure. He was much more a man of action than a silk-wearing fop. He didn't enjoy the clothes he had to wear—they were a far cry from his normal rough adventurer's tunics and cloaks, which he liked all hung about with shields and weapons. These silks and satins tended to ride up and the silk stockings twisted themselves all around his beefy legs. And the shoes had little heels like some silly girl's shoes; tottering about on them would be no fun, either.

CHAPTER 18

Some Days Later, the Palace Ballroom, 8 P.M.

The night of the ball arrived. The sinister servant in black was efficiency itself as the palace and the gardens were transformed and decorated. There were Chinese lanterns hung in the trees and there were candles and garlands of roses. There was a huge crowd of very overdressed and snobbish people in the ballroom by the time Prince Charming made his great entrance. Jake put his best foot forward, swallowed his pride, and almost fell headlong down the grand staircase on his silly, high, pinching shoes. Oh, for a pair of good seven-league boots, he thought as he straightened up with a fixed smile on his handsome face. He soon recovered and danced with several of the grand young ladies. They all, of course, danced with great style and professionalism, but there was no interest and no spark between any of them and the prince.

Jake was very bored by now with his tedious duties as Prince Charming. He had wanted to play the dashing prince, of course, but not like this, not foppishly dressed in silk hose, and hiding behind a black velvet mask. He had danced dutifully with all the eligible ladies in the kingdom, and also with one or two who were perhaps not so eligible. There were two in particular with a very pushy mother, who were constantly drawing attention to themselves and making moony eyes at him. He had danced with each of them once, surely that was more than enough and beyond the call of story duty.

Then there was a sudden fanfare of trumpets and the doors opened at the top of the ballroom steps. A girl appeared in shimmering gray silk. She tripped lightly down the stairs and all eyes followed this new, ravishingly beautiful and mysterious arrival. Jake noticed that on her dainty feet she wore little crystal glass slippers; that was the sign he was waiting for. He approached the lovely girl and bowed in his most elegant manner. He felt suddenly, somehow, very cheered up. They danced and danced together, hour after hour it seemed, whirling around and around to the music.

The Palace Ballroom
11:45 P.M.

After many dances together Jake offered to fetch her a glass of refreshing champagne and she sweetly nodded her assent. He went out to the terrace and waited while his steward went to fetch two chilled flute glasses. He hoped the lovely girl would soon come out and join him. He looked at the moon, and the stars, and the deep blue of the sky and said to himself, "I am in love. I have to admit it. It's ridiculous, but there it is. What on earth can be happening to me? It's just the sort of thing our mother is always warning us about."

The Terrace of the Palace
11:59 P.M. and 56 seconds, precisely

The palace clock whirred and clicked as it geared up for midnight. Soon there would be the great fireworks display. Jake leaned on the balustrade and breathed in the jasmine-scented air. All his faculties seemed to be heightened: touch, taste, smell, and sight. Sadly his hearing was not so affected, or he would have heard someone creeping up behind him on the terrace. The next thing he was aware of was an odd sweet sickly smell layered on top of the perfume of the jasmine. As he breathed it in, the clanging bells of the clock chimes sounded somehow blurred and strangely wavery. He tried counting along with the chimes of the clock as he waited for the first rocket to be launched in its haze of golden sparks.

Ding nine, *Ding* eleventy,
Ding three, *Ding* sixty-four . . .

Something was very, very, very wrong. The last thing he could remember hearing before he woke up in a distant, dark, and very deep dungeon, was the voice of the girl in the glass slippers, the new love of his life, crying out from somewhere far away, "Oh no!" as he fell down and slipped into a deep sleep on the palace terrace.

CHAPTER 19

The Southern Lands
Some Days Later, 11 A.M.

Tom and the crow made good progress as they
walked down the pretty southern road from the
crossroads near Snoreing. It was a pleasant stroll
among all the baby rabbits, the squirrels, and the fluting little bluebirds. Suddenly one of the pretty birds
dropped an envelope at Tom's feet and then flew off. It
was from the Story Bureau and was addressed to Tom.
He opened it. Inside was just a tiny square of paper, on
which was written:

Dear Tom Trueheart,

This is a copy of the clue that we believe was sent to your brother Jake. "Travel south, you will find a land that is very neat and well kept. Look out for a girl wearing glass slippers."

Sincerely,

The Story Bureau

Tom read the message out to the crow. "Would you say we were in a neat land?" Tom asked.

"I think we'll know it when we see it," said the crow.

They walked until later in the afternoon when they both noticed something about the outskirts of the little town that they were approaching. For the first time they realized that perhaps they had found themselves in a very neat place.

"This must be neatness," said Tom looking around at the houses they were passing. They were tall and gray and white. It looked as if one puff of wind, just the slightest of breezes, would blow them away completely. The front gardens of the houses had very neatly laid-out straight rows of spindly trees trimmed and clipped into tight neat triangular shapes. The trees looked as if they were made of the thinnest flattest cardboard. They passed whole avenues of houses and mansions and gardens, and all of them had the same refined and very neat and tidy appearance.

"Looks very neat to me," said the crow. "If this place *isn't* neat, I don't know what is."

"I think this means we are there, all right," said Tom. "Now we just have to find someone with glass slippers on their feet."

"Oh, I should think they are two a penny round here," said the crow. "Look at her, for instance."

On the other side of the avenue a woman was walking with a tiny dog. She wore a high gray wig piled on her head. At the very top of the wig was a tiny straw hat with a little silk bird perched shakily on it. Her dress was very narrow at the waist but very full and wide in the skirt so that she looked like a very fancy lampshade. She carried a shepherd's crook with a pink ribbon tied to it and a tiny dog on a lead made of fine sprite ribbon, also in pink. The dog wore a coat of the same pattern as the woman's dress.

"Now, I wouldn't be at all surprised if she had glass slippers on under there," said the crow.

"Really?" said Tom. "I can't exactly go and ask her, can I?"

"Not really," said the crow, "but you must admit this is a very, very neat and very tidy-looking place."

They soon reached the center of the very elegant little town. Tom had never seen such an ordered place. He was used to simple rustic wooden houses tucked into clearings in forests, all overgrown with soft green moss and dark ivy. There were always woodcutters and soldiers and wicked hairy wolves and wicked hairy farmers and brave hairy adventurers. Here the houses were all done up in gold, or were white limestone, or rose pink brick. All the trees and shrubs were either trimmed and cut into silly fancy shapes, or stuck into big flowerpots outside the front doors and gates of the houses. The cobbles were gray and neat, and every so often a grand carriage and horses would sweep by the pair of them. There were teams of lowly people in the road wearing aprons who were just there to pick up horse poo with little silver shovels; that's how neat it all was!

Tom felt very scruffy, and they were certainly getting some strange looks from the people they passed, perhaps on account of Jollity the crow, who was riding happily on Tom's shoulder. As they crossed an avenue lined with elegant shops he suddenly flew off and perched high up on a sign.

"What are you doing now, Crow? Come on, you can't just sit up there looking like a pretty picture," said Tom.

"Look at the sign," said the crow cagily, speaking quite quietly out of the side of its beak.

Tom looked up. The sign hung from an elaborate iron bracket that was made up of twisty curlicues and shapes. It was a square of elegantly turned wood with the word COFFEEHOUSE painted on it.

"Well," said Tom, puzzled, "it's a coffeehouse, whatever that means."

"People go in there and drink cups of coffee," said the crow, "but that's not the point. Look at the picture on the sign."

Tom looked again, and sure enough there was a dainty painting of a glass shoe, a lady's shoe with a fashionable kitten heel and a fancy glass buckle.

"Glass slippers on her feet," said Tom. "Come on, let's find out what this means."

"You go in, Tom," said the crow. "I'm not sure I'll be welcome in a fancy-pants place like that." So Jollity the crow waited on the hanging sign, while Tom pushed open the door of the coffeehouse and went inside.

It was certainly bustling in the coffee shop. All kinds of characters sat at little tables drinking from tiny elegant cups. Among them Tom saw a king who was actually wearing his crown and reading a parchment newssheet. Then there was a very pretty girl in ash gray clothes, who had smuts of soot and smudges of dirt all over her face. She was talking to a large furry bear in a tweed waistcoat.

"But you see," she was saying, "I had it all: beautiful clothes, a gray silk dress and cape, tiara, all magically given fair and square by my very own and I must say very odd-looking Fairy Godmother. 'Make sure you are back by midnight,' she said. Well, I fell in love, didn't I, for goodness' sake? Just on midnight and it was all going so well. I had been dancing with a very dishy prince and I am sure he was falling for me, too. The clock started to strike midnight, it was my own fault, I know I was warned, but anyway I went out onto the terrace for a romantic glass of champagne with the prince, I couldn't resist, and what did I see? The poor prince being kidnapped, yes kidnapped, if you please. The fireworks went off, and while the rockets were exploding and everyone was going *ooh* and *ahh*, I was trying to tell all the useless flunkies that the poor prince had been spirited away. The clock struck midnight with a great big clang and all my fine clothes simply vanished. There I was back in these rags. Well, of course, I ran off as fast as I could, I can tell you. I tripped up and left one of my glass slippers behind. For some reason those dear little shoes didn't vanish."

"You told me all this yesterday," said the big bear, staring gloomily into his cup.

Tom kept very quiet and just listened, hoping not to be noticed.

"Everything's gone very strange lately," said the bear. "That awful girl is still in our house, can't get her out, the wife's very upset, and as for that tiny wee bear, well, we've been properly lumbered with him. He's no relation at all to us and he's a little pain at the best of times. He's nothing but trouble and barely house-trained, and now he won't stop teasing us and mucking about. It's all in the story contract, so that's who we have to work with. I don't know what the Bureau is going to do about it."

"That's my point," said the ash-faced girl. "You can't have princes kidnapped like that for no reason. He was just an innocent adventurer out doing his best, then he's bundled off by some weird creep. Not the way it should all work as a story, is it, I ask you? That's not a proper ending."

Tom listened, stunned. An innocent adventurer, a glass slipper: surely she must mean Jake. This girl must be part of Jake's story. A story that was interrupted by a kidnap. This was surely proof at last that something bad and dangerous really had happened to his brothers.

Tom finally spoke up. "Sorry, miss," he said, "but I couldn't help overhearing you. My name is Tom Trueheart, and I am on a mission to find my missing brothers. They are all adventurers and I am, too, in a way, although only an apprentice. I think that the man you saw being kidnapped could well have been my big brother Jake."

"Jake," said the girl. "Well now, that is a fine manly sort of name. He was certainly broad enough for a name like that. We were told that he was called Prince Charming, but there was no first name, of course. I had grown so very fond of him, too."

The bear shook his great hairy head.

"You see, Thomas," the girl continued, "my poor father has married an awful sort of woman with two very horrible daughters. All I do is run around after them all day and clean the house."

The hairy bear stood up suddenly muttering, "If I've heard this once, I've heard it twenty times," and he blundered off, squeezing his big hairy bottom past all the dainty tables.

"They call me Cinderella at home," the lovely girl continued, "and they think that's no end of a joke because I am covered in ash all day from cleaning out their awful dirty fireplaces. I really need to escape from my life and soon. That nice prince, if he really was your brother, was my best hope. If you manage to find him, please send him back to rescue me. I'm sure he could find a way. He seemed so big and so brave and so strong." And she sniffed as a tear dropped into her coffee cup.

"I'll do my best, miss," he said. "I'll find a way—I am a Trueheart, after all."

A man in an apron with a tray of delicate cups balanced on his arm tapped Tom on the shoulder.

"Can I serve you anything at all, my noble young sir?" he said with a sneering expression. "Or are you just passing through here on your way to somewhere less fashionable?"

"I'm leaving now, sir," Tom said. "Don't worry," he said to the pretty ash-faced girl, "I'll sort it all out. I'll sneak off to the palace garden and look for clues; I'll find him for you."

She leaned forward and grabbed his arm. "Make sure that you do, for my sake," she whispered. "I'm not sure I can carry on with this terrible life of cleaning and scrubbing and so on. I need rescuing, and I really do love him."

With that, Tom reassured her and scampered back out to the street. A little crowd of overdressed people had gathered looking up at the crow high on its perch over the coffee shop.

"That bird is quite spoiling the charm of the sign," said one.

"An ugly creature," said another.

"Someone told me that it speaks."

"Really, a bewitched crow on the loose. I don't know what the Story Bureau thinks they are doing these days, I'm sure." And with that, the particular dandy blew his nose loudly into a pink silk handkerchief.

"Come on, Crow," said Tom.

The crow flew down and landed on Tom's shoulder, and the overdressed crowd made a path for the young adventurer and his companion.

"I think he is a warlock," whispered one.

"Don't look him in the eye," said another.

"Looks like he's got fleas," said a third. "The bird, that is."

The crow turned its head to the crowd and made as loud a raspberry noise as a crow can manage through a beak.

Tom and Jollity made their way to the palace gardens. The crow flew up and down over the grass lawns and hedges, hoping to catch sight of something in the way of a clue.

"No signs yet?" asked Tom.

"Nothing to report," said the crow. "Wait, Tom, I can see something sparkly under that hedge by the steep steps."

Tom walked over and poked about in the trimmed bushes; his hand touched something smooth and cold. He pulled out a tiny delicate glass shoe. It was an elegant lady's evening slipper with a kitten heel. He held it carefully in his hands.

"It's just like that girl was saying; she dropped a glass slipper when she ran away."

"I should be careful with that," said the crow. "It's

evidence, and it looks like it might break very easily."

"You're right, Crow," said Tom, and he carefully wrapped the slipper in the soft warm cloak in his adventurer's travel bag.

"We'll carry this with us. This a real clue. You never know, but I think that might come in very useful at some point," he said, and they set off.

CHAPTER 20

Jacques's Story
Some Weeks Before, in the Northeast Kingdom
Zero degrees Celsius, 4:25 P.M.

Jacques's Story Bureau letter (hung from sprite ribbon on a lamp above the stairs), sent him to the far and remote northeast of the Land of Stories. He walked through blizzards and driving cold winds, then one evening he saw a warm-looking little house tucked away in a line of trees. It reminded him of home. It had a chimney that billowed white smoke, and a friendly light shone out from the windows; it looked very inviting. This seems like as good a place as any, thought Jacques, as he shivered in the cold. He knocked on the stout wooden door, which was soon opened. A little man, more of a dwarf, really, looked up at him with a worried expression.

"Good evening, traveler," he said.

"May I come in for a while and warm myself? I have been traveling these last two days and nights and it looks set to be another cold raw night tonight," said Jacques.

"You may come in," said the little man, "but I should warn you, we are all armed."

Jacques crouched down and entered the little house. "Jacques Trueheart, adventurer," he said.

"Hi, Jacques," came a chorus of voices, for there were more of the little men.

"There seem to be so many of you," Jacques said as they crowded the doorway.

"There are a good few of us, it's true," said one of them. "We all work in the big diamond mine together, all seven of us."

"Seven of us, all right," said one, a smiling fellow, "just one big happy family."

"Well, we were happy once," said a gloomy-looking little man with a loud sniff. "Not any more."

"That's true, we were a bigger happy family once, not so long ago."

"I see," said Jacques. "Well, I am an adventurer sent to follow a story in this area. Perhaps I could help you?"

"I fear it's too late for any help. If only you had arrived a few days ago."

"Why, what happened?" asked Jacques.

"It's a long story. Settle yourself down before the fire, young man, have some supper, and then I will tell you."

So Jacques settled himself in a comfortable chair by the fire and the little man told his story.

"We had a very wicked queen in this northern place. She was a cruel sorceress among other things, and she was very jealous of her lovely stepdaughter, Snow White. She sent a huntsman out one day to kill the poor girl, and she told him to bring back the girl's heart as proof.

The hunter couldn't bring himself to do it. He told Snow White to run away, and he killed a wild boar instead and took the bloody heart to show the queen.

"Snow White found our little house and she lived here with us; she took care of us and we protected her. The wicked queen had a magic sprite mirror and she found out that Snow White was still alive after all. She disguised herself and she found Snow White here and fed her an enchanted apple. When Snow White ate the apple she fell into an enchanted sleep, and only the kiss of true love can waken her. We chased the wicked queen and she fell to her death in an icy ravine. Then we took our lovely Snow White and we made a special crystal coffin and hid her somewhere very safe."

Jacques sat back, amazed. This surely was his story. He was to be the chosen one who would waken Snow White.

"Will you take me to this secret place?" said Jacques. "I am sure now that it is my destiny to wake the lovely Snow White from her sleep of death; I was sent to play the prince."

"I don't know," said the storyteller, whose name was Joe. "Can we trust you?" He looked around at his six brothers. "What do we think?" he said.

"It's a funny thing," Jacques said, "but I have six brothers as well, and your little house here reminds me so much of my home: same cozy atmosphere, books, wood fires, all gathered together telling stories like this."

"He's got six brothers," said Joe.

"He must be all right, then," said another.

"I'll take you," said Joe. "We leave at first light."

The next morning Joe and Jacques took their leave of the others. Jacques shook hands with all six who remained behind, and then, wrapping himself in his winter cloak and hoisting his packstaff, he walked with Joe out into the snow.

They had not gone much farther on their eastward journey when they met up with another traveler on the road. A tall man muffled up in a long black cloak, who was trudging through the snow in the same direction. He fell in with the two travelers, and kindly little Joe led them on a complicated route across the dangerous countryside. Joe was used to the drifts of snow, the ravines, and the lofty crags of this wild place, for which the tall dark-cloaked stranger was grateful. When Jacques thought that they were at last hopelessly lost, little Joe took off his hat. He gestured for the other two men to do the same. They had reached a grove, a semicircle of spruce trees. The tops of the trees were white with snow, but the dense lower branches were still deep dark green. The boughs made a mesh of interlocking arms, a kind of protective roof. Below, raised on a natural outcrop of rock, was a long glass box. Joe turned to the two men and indicated without speaking that they should follow him. He walked very slowly forward in the deep snow, and Jacques and the tall man in black followed him until they were standing by the glass box. Snow White lay inside. Her skin was white as snow, her lips were the color of bright blood, and her hair was as dark as a raven's wing. Jacques was instantly smitten with love. His heart broke to see the lovely girl so perfect and deeply asleep in her enchantment. He wanted to touch her, to stroke her hair, to place a kiss on that pale cheek. He asked Joe to lift the lid of the glass coffin.

The man in the black cloak whispered, "I will do it; I have the height and strength, after all."

Joe said angrily, "I may be a dwarf, but I am stronger than ten of you ordinary men." He leaned forward, unlocked the clasp on the glass lid, and raised it on its golden hinges.

"A fine piece of work," said the man in black.

"Shhh," Joe said, in a fury now with the sinister stranger and wishing he hadn't allowed him to tag along with them. "Show some respect."

Jacques knelt by the open coffin and looked at the face of Snow White—so pale, so pure—and love swelled in his heart. He leaned forward to plant a kiss on Snow White's cheek. Before he reached her face he was aware of her perfume. It was a sweet smell, perhaps too sweet, like a bowl of overblown roses that have stood too long in the sun. His head swam and he felt weak suddenly. He heard a cold, quiet whispered voice very close in his ear.

"I used the same drug on our little dwarf friend here, and your brothers, too, Mr. so-called adventurer Trueheart, each one of them so far as hopeless as yourself. What a collection of brawny fools. How very easy it has all been."

Jacques could not even speak now. He just stared ahead in horror, realizing that the love of his young life, this Snow White, who was his Juliet, his Cleopatra, his Helen, had no protection now at all. He just managed to catch a glimpse of little Joe slumped beside him, perhaps dead, before he himself fell into a deep sleep, down onto the welcoming soft snow.

CHAPTER 21

Tom on the Road
11 A.M.

Tom carried the satchel with the little glass shoe inside it very carefully. It was a fine morning, the sun shone brightly, and the birds were singing. The crow was in a "flying on ahead" kind of mood. Every so often Tom caught up with him and they managed a little chat together before the bird flew away again, on down the straight road north.

"I wonder what's really happened to all my brothers, where they are, and why are they there?"

"Someone evil is surely holding them prisoner," said the

crow. "The Master said to be very careful, and so we should."

"An evil villain, all right," said Tom. "And how much do you know about it all, anyway, Jollity?"

"Can't tell you that," said the crow. "That would be helping. I can just say that we should be very careful of whoever we meet. You're on a special mission from the Master, and whoever is doing this is obviously trying to destroy the Master and everyone and everything in the Land of Stories."

"Imagine if we had no stories," said Tom.

"Don't even think about it," said the crow. "We all need stories. Why, do you know, Tom, I've seen people waiting in great long lines outside one of the Story Bureau bookshops to read all about one of your big brothers and their latest adventures, when the books are first published—whole long lines stretching all the way down the street."

"Really," said Tom, "all the way down the street?"

"All the way down the street, outside the bookshop itself, and then right round the corner and beyond—

especially when *Jack the Giant Killer* was published," said the crow.

Tom found it hard to imagine such a faraway world, miles beyond the woods and forests and mountains of the Land of Stories. A busy place where people led everyday lives, and on their journeys to and from work, or at the end of the day, would read all about his father or one of his brothers. Perhaps in the evenings, gathered around their own cozy firesides, and instead of being able to listen to the actual brothers telling the story face-to-face as Tom could, they would picture it happening, and hear the storyteller's voice in their heads by reading the story to themselves or even out loud to one another. He supposed that was what the book was printed for, so that everyone everywhere could enjoy a good adventure story and read the storyteller's adventure in his own words as he lived it; it was simple, really. Now some evil person was out to stop all the fun forever.

They walked on for two days and nights, and at some

point they seemed to have crossed a border. They found themselves somewhere very cold.

"We must be in the far north by now," said Jollity. "It's certainly cold enough, brr."

Tom wrapped himself up in Jackie's winter cloak and was glad of it. He kept the glass slipper safe by wrapping it up in the Trueheart bundle cloth.

They carried on, encountering snow and howling winds. As darkness fell they saw a light off the road in a grove of trees. They found the sheltered spot only to discover six dwarfs with lanterns, pickaxes, weapons, and shovels, standing around a crystal coffin. Tom could see a beautiful girl, with pale skin and black hair, fast asleep in the glass box. The dwarfs were sniffling and weeping as they dug a deep hole.

"Forgive us, sir, if we carry on," one of the tearful little men said, "but we must finish this terrible job before nightfall."

"Who is that in there?" Tom asked.

"That is the lovely Snow White. She has been in an

enchanted sleep and may only be woken by the kiss of true love. A noble traveler came along and we thought he would be able to wake her. Our brother Joe set off with him to come here. That was an age ago and we have not seen them since. When we came here to find them, we found only this, Joe's short sword lying in the snow." He picked up a broad, short weapon and held it above his head where the lantern light gleamed off the fine edge.

"She remains in her sleep of death, her last chance gone. So we are burying her in this sacred place forever." The little man sighed and then plunged his shovel into the cold earth again.

"Wait," said Tom. "I am on a quest, looking for my lost brothers. What was the name of this traveler?"

"Jacques, as I recall," said the little man. "A fine-looking young adventurer, I should say."

"That is one of my brothers, my friend. He is surely meant to wake her. The crow here and I are following clues and we will find him, have no fear. My name is Thomas Trueheart of the adventuring Truehearts, and nothing will stop me. I will bring him back here to waken this girl, so please, I beg you all, don't bury her."

"What do you think, lads?"

"It would do no harm to wait a little longer. I would rather anything but this awful final burying," said one of them from inside the hole.

"I agree. Let's give the boy a chance to bring him back."

"Are we agreed, then?"

"Agreed," they all chorused.

"You'd best come back with us, young man, and get a hot meal inside you."

Tom and the crow spent a comfortable night with the six dwarfs in their cozy house. Stories were told around the fireside before bed; Tom told them all that had happened to him.

In the morning, before Tom and Jollity set off, the dwarfs insisted that Tom take Joe's sword with him.

"If you find your brother you'll find Joe as well, and if what you say is true, you will need a fierce defender and a good weapon."

So Tom buckled on his first real sword under the winter cloak. And as he walked the long road east through the Land of Stories, he felt even more like a real adventurer than ever.

CHAPTER 22

Jackson's Story
The Eastern Gate, the Eastern Lands, 9:00 P.M.

Jackson had set out on his journey in worried spirits. His story letter had upset him more than he would admit. There was not even a hint of romance to come, only slime and wet and suffering. At the Eastern Gate it was hard to make out anything at all, the visibility was so bad. The gate itself loomed up in the fog. It was made of willow sticks and gnarled and twisted branches all braided together. The gatekeeper scuttled out of his lean-to shack to raise the barrier for Jackson, doffed his cap to him, and said, "Welcome to the land of witches, warlocks, spells, and enchanters, Mr. Trueheart. You are expected. I have you down on my list for a transformation; frog, is it not?"

"Yes it is. Come on, then, get it over with," said Jackson.

"Ooh no, bless you, I'm only the gatekeeper. This sprite will sort you out, and good luck to you, sir." He was shortly joined, as if from nowhere, by a wood sprite dressed in usual sprite fashion: leaves and moss and bits of twig and greenery all over.

"Turned out very damp again, hasn't it?" he said to Jackson.

"Yes, it certainly has," said Jackson politely.

"Name of Trueheart, is it, first name Jackson?" said the sprite, peering at a piece of tattered paper in the gloom. "I take it that you are fully aware of an enchantment to be carried out, and that you are indeed Jackson Trueheart, already named under Rule Five, and that you have indeed been so chosen."

"I am," said Jackson.

"That, furthermore, by reading your original letter of instruction you have agreed in principle to the said transformation, to wit, one frog."

"Agreed," said Jackson.

"Right, then," said the sprite. "By virtue of the powers invested in me by the Story Bureau, and for the purposes of the current story, as already agreed, I hereby carry out a transformation. I should hang on to something, if I were you; in my experience people often come over a little queasy during this part of the process.

I therefore hereby declare that you, Jackson Trueheart, designated adventurer, pro tem prince of the realm, will now undergo enchantment number eleven, seven, six, nine, as agreed etc., etc., under those terms."

Jackson did feel a moment of queasiness. He closed his eyes. "Is that it?" he said.

"You'll have to speak up," said the sprite. "You are rather a long way away and also very small."

Jackson opened his eyes. The world looked, sounded, and smelled very different. A giant stood a little way off, towering over him. Goodness, I really am a frog, Jackson thought.

The suddenly-huge sprite picked Jackson up so that Jackson's back legs and webbed feet flopped and dangled. He took Jackson over to a bridge and held him out over the water.

"Well now," said the sprite, "I do declare the enchantment to be complete and satisfactory. As a last little bit of help, and strictly against the rules, I'll just pop you into the water, Your Highness. Ta-ta for now."

CHAPTER 23

In a Puddle of Dirty Water

Jackson hit the water with a splash, so that his first cry of "*riddip*" was drowned out by the noise. He quickly surfaced and found that he could swim almost effortlessly, and that now and then his tongue flicked out unasked and snagged a tasty morsel or two on the wing. After filling himself up with bugs and creepy crawlies, Jackson eventually fell fast asleep on a lily pad.

He woke into his new world as a frog, and after swimming and flopping about in the muddy water happily for a while, he came to a long, high wall. He supposed that this was the outer garden wall of a palace. Jackson hopped through the railings of a small side gate and slid into a huge and well-tended garden. The garden was full of sunshine and flowers, and tall trees and statues.

A beautiful young girl stood near a well. She was playing catch with a golden ball. She threw the ball high into the air and caught it, over and over, as Jackson watched. Jackson was smitten, and in a single instant, with deep love.

There was a sudden anguished cry from the girl. She had missed the catch. Her golden ball had fallen into the mouth of the well and had dropped deep down into the dark water.

"Oh, help, someone, please," she called out pitifully.

Jackson at once called out to her, "I'll help you, never fear, your loveliness, your utter beautifulness." Of course, she was so far away on the other side of the garden that she couldn't hear him; he was just a tiny frog, after all, among many other tiny creatures.

"Oh please, someone. I must have my precious golden ball back. I will give anything to get it. Surely someone must be able to help me. I will do anything," she cried.

Jackson hopped over to the well head, made a giant leap using his long back legs and landed right in front of her on the slippery rim of the well.

"Ugh," she said disgustedly.

"*Riddip, riddip.* Sorry, I mean, I'm here to help," said the frog as loudly as he could manage.

"Of course you are, you seriously disgusting thing, now go away."

"I'll fetch your golden ball for you," said Jackson the brave adventurer, the frog prince.

"Will you, now," said the girl. "And what, pray, will you expect from me in return?"

"A lover's kiss?" said Jackson hopefully. "Your hand in marriage?"

She burst out laughing. "Well," she said, "you do have a sense of humor, at least, and talking frogs are fairly rare on the ground around here. I'll tell you what, you go down into that slimy, dark, disgusting well and fetch me back my very precious ball and, of course, I will marry you."

So it was that Jackson Trueheart, the brave frog prince, dived into the dark water among the filthy slimy weeds, all for the love of a beautiful girl. He found the ball easily enough; it was caught up in some weeds. Jackson untangled the ball and took it up to the surface of the well. It was a short climb to the lip, and although the ball was made of gold, the metal had been beaten and worked very thin, so that it was almost, but not quite, as light as air. Jackson returned the ball to the princess, who was delighted to have it back.

"Thank you so much, Mr. Frog," she said. "Perhaps you will do me the honor of dining with my father, the king, and me this evening."

So, thought Jackson, she is a princess as well.

"I should be delighted, Your Highness, *riddip*," said Jackson and he even tried to make a little bow, which was difficult for a frog-shaped prince.

The princess, at the table with her father, the king, was unusually quiet that evening.

"Whatever is the matter, my dear?" said the king.

"I lost my golden ball down the well today and a talking frog fetched it back for me."

"A talking frog, eh? Now that is something that I should very much like to see."

"Well, that's the trouble, Father. I fear you will meet him and soon. I made a rash promise to this frog: he asked me to marry him before he would go and fetch the ball."

"And?" said the king.

"And I agreed. I had to have that ball and I promised. I invited him to dinner first, and now I fear he will come. He's an ugly green slimy thing. Ugh," she said.

"Well, my dear," said the king, secretly amused, "a promise is a promise."

The king's servant brought in a flagon of wine. He was a tall thin man in black with a full head of white hair. He bowed low as he placed the wine on the table. Any room seemed a few degrees colder whenever this particular servant was in it.

"That will be all."

"Yes, sire," said the servant, bowing low, and giving a disturbing smile as he left.

"I don't like that man," said the princess.

The king put his finger to his lips. "Shhh, my dear," he said. "Have a care, he might hear you. I don't like him, either, but good servants are hard to come by in this benighted age."

In the echoing quiet of the palace they suddenly heard the sound of four tiny damp feet, *slip-slopping* down the stone corridor, *slip-slop, slip-slop*. In a moment the heavy door swung just the tiniest bit open, and there was Jackson the frog prince.

"Good evening, Your Highnesses," he croaked.

"Well, well, so you really are a talking frog," said the king. "Welcome, my friend, and pray join us at the table."

Jackson tried as best he could to eat the fine supper

daintily, but he was, after all, a frog: he could only gobble and slurp with his long tongue until he was nicely full. "Burp, *riddip*, burp," he said.

The princess wrinkled up her pretty nose in disgust. However, to her surprise, she found that the frog was at least a good talker and he did his best to amuse them both during supper. The king seemed to enjoy the frog's company and after a while the princess did, too. Jackson was at his wittiest, regaling them with all sorts of stories, quoting romantic poetry, and generally being the life and soul of the party.

After supper, the king, secretly delighted at his daughter's suitor, even encouraged Jackson to go with the princess to her chamber.

Jackson hopped up beside her and looked longingly at the princess, at her beautiful elegant head and her golden hair spread across the pillow.

"Ah, me," he sighed, "if only I could give you a good-night kiss."

"If I give you just one little peck on the cheek,

would that please you?" the princess asked.

Jackson could hardly believe his luck, a kiss so soon. He knew the pattern of Story Bureau enchantment stories well enough to think that such a kiss might be enough to break his spell. Jackson hopped closer on the pillow, as near as he could to her lovely face. The princess closed her eyes and pursed her beautiful scarlet lips. She was about to kiss the charming frog prince when the bedroom door swung open and the king's second footman and table servant whispered like dark smoke into the room. He reached his long thin arm across the bed, snatched Jackson from the pillow, and stuffed him into his deep black pocket. Jackson let out a muffled cry of "*riddip*," and before the princess could even open her eyes, the servant and the frog had seemingly melted away and vanished into the dark.

CHAPTER 24

In Which Tom and the Crow
Meet a Distressed Princess

While they walked together Tom and the crow were joined on the road by a sprite. He slipped out of the trees, and was so cleverly disguised that at first Tom had a shock and thought that even the trees could walk and talk in the Land of Stories.

"Good morning to you," said the sprite, and he raised his leaf cap in greeting.

"Good morning," said Tom. "Are you a sprite?"

"I can't answer that, young man, as I'm sure you must be aware; my business is my own."

This sprite was obviously a bit of a stickler for all the rules and regulations. He seemed cheerful enough, though. Tom knew perfectly well that this was a sprite by his clothes, and as far as he knew, this was the first sprite that he had ever met.

"My name's Tom Trueheart," said Tom, "and this is . . . er . . . my friend Crow."

"Trueheart, you say." The sprite looked thoughtful. "Do you know, I met your brother not far from here a while back. Nice-looking young man, all dressed in green."

"Yes, that's Jackson," said Tom. "He is one of my brothers; I've got six of them altogether. They are all missing and we are on a quest to find them and rescue them."

"Quest, rescue: dangerous words for a young fellow like you to use," said the sprite.

"That's my job," said Tom. "Where exactly did you see him, and when?"

"Let's put it this way," said the sprite. "I held him up, and I dropped him in."

"Dropped him in where?" said Tom, alarmed.

"Why," said the sprite with a wink, "in the river over there, *riddip*." With that the sprite dissolved back among the bushes and trees without a sound, as if he had never been there.

"Of course," said Tom, "Jackson was to be a frog. That sprite must have enchanted Jackson; he was the one who turned him into a frog."

They set off to follow the course of the river. The crow flew on from time to time and scouted ahead. After an hour or so he came back.

"There's a fine palace up ahead, Tom; we should head that way."

As they neared the garden wall of the palace they met

a pretty young woman. She was dressed in a cloak and had a travel-size crown on her head and a small case in her hand.

Tom bowed low as she approached. "Good afternoon, Your Highness," he said.

"Oh yes, well, good afternoon to you, good, well done," she replied distractedly.

"Are you off on an adventure?" Tom asked.

"An adventure? I suppose I am, really." She put her case down, and it made a clank as it touched the ground.

"I am setting off to find a suitable young man to marry," she said. "I was doing very well, playing catch in my garden, pleasing myself, and then something happened and I have become discontented with my lot, even though I am a princess."

"What happened?" Tom asked her.

"You wouldn't believe me if I told you," she said. "You will think I am mad."

"Try me," said Tom.

"Well, I lost my beautiful golden ball down a well and

a talking frog rescued it for me. For a joke I said I would marry him. Do you know, I grew quite fond of him; he was good company and liked poetry."

"Really?" said Tom.

"Really. And he had such good conversational skills. He was sophisticated and witty, qualities I had been missing in my silly selfish life. I was about to kiss him, of all things, when he vanished, just walked off and left me. Ever since I have been troubled. I need to find a good husband just like that frog. Now you do think me mad, admit it."

"No, I don't, Your Highness. I think we can help you, me and my friend the crow here. We are on a quest to find just such a frog as you describe. Don't dash off and marry any old person on the rebound. Why not wait a bit and I will bring him back to you? I fear he is possibly under an enchantment."

"Now that would explain a lot," said the princess.

"When we find him we will bring him straight to you, I promise."

"Bless you," she said. "What is your name, if I may ask?"

"I am Tom Trueheart of the adventuring Truehearts, at your service," Tom said.

"Go with all good speed and find my frog. Here, take this with you." She opened her case and pulled out a beautiful golden ball as light as spun sugar. "This might prove very useful for an adventurer: sprite gold," she said, "worth a king's ransom. You never know."

Tom took the beautiful ball and tucked it into his bag with the glass slipper. "Never fear, Your Highness," he said. "We will return with both the ball and the frog."

CHAPTER 25

A House in the Woods

After some hours on the road they turned off onto a forest path. Tom pulled the map out of his bag and they studied the area: just forest and roads and smaller byways and paths that crisscrossed through the trees. There was a tiny cottage marked not so very far from where they stood, in a clearing of the forest. They were surrounded now by big oak trees, and the last of the low sun gilded the leaves and trunks. It also helpfully lit up a twisty path through the trees that looked almost inviting enough to follow. Tom, reluctantly but much encouraged by Jollity the crow, set off down the path.

After a while they came to the clearing and there stood the little house. Something about the cottage gave Tom the shivers. It was very unusual looking. It had a white roof as if it were covered in snow, and there were blobs of something brightly colored in red and green sticking out of the white. As they got closer to the house Tom noticed an odd smell. The house smelled of something delicious and sweet. It smelled of gingerbread.

When they were close enough Tom reached out to one of the walls, which looked like a dark roughcast brown concrete, but when he actually touched it, it felt soft. Tom pulled a piece of the wall away. It came off very easily and Tom sniffed it and touched it to his tongue. It tasted of gingerbread. It was gingerbread.

Tom realized in an instant how very hungry he was. He tore out a big chunk of the wall and ate it greedily. Then he ate some more, and then some more, until he was full. The crow flew down from the roof with a big chunk of red candy in its beak.

"That roof is covered in sugar icing, and now I know what this place is," he said.

"Really?" said Tom.

"This is the Gingerbread House from that old story of Hansel and Gretel. Do you remember it? Hansel and Gretel must have been lost in this very forest."

"My mum told me that story when I was little," said Tom. "Of course, the house was just like this in the picture book: the candies, the candy canes, and everything." Tom suddenly felt ill; his head swam and it was not from eating too much gingerbread. It was a sudden memory. A memory of the cruel and vicious witch who had featured in that story. A witch who had cooked and eaten children. Tom at once set off back down the darkening path.

"Where are you going? What's the hurry?" said the crow.

"I think you know the answer to that," Tom called hurriedly over his shoulder. "There is a nasty, evil, child-eating witch very near here and I'm not waiting

around to meet up with her, thank you."

"Tom, wait a minute, come back. That witch has long gone—she went up in a puff of smoke at the end of the story, remember?"

"Did she?" said Tom.

"This is just the place where the story happened. It was years ago now," said the crow. "A relative of mine was involved in it; I remember hearing about it directly from him."

"Was he one of those birds that ate the crumbs that Hansel and Gretel dropped? I remember them," said Tom.

"One of those birds . . . yes, that's it, he was one of those birds, and he was . . . er . . . an old uncle of mine," stammered the crow. "Let's go inside the house and sleep.

I mean, how bad can it be? And it's getting very dark very quickly, and we need to rest."

Tom at least dared to open the front door of the gingerbread cottage, which was a big step for him to take, seeing how scared of the dark he normally was. The door protested and creaked alarmingly, as if it hadn't been opened for years and years. The hinges squealed and shrieked, and then the door was fully open. It was very dark and very quiet inside the house. Tom found one of his mother's useful candle stubs and some matches in his bag. He lit the candle, and in the sudden warm light he saw that everything inside the little gingerbread house was very strange and very pointy. There were high pointy-edged windows, and the pointy glass in them seemed to be made of thin barley sugar. There were pointy chairs and even a pointy table, with pointy legs, and on the table was an abandoned and dusty tall pointy black hat. There was a big iron stove with dark pointy doors, and even a pointy chimney. Tom shivered.

"This place is very creepy and very pointy," he said.

"Well, it was a witch's house, after all," said the crow.

Tom looked up the dark twisty stairs. He could see a pointy bedroom door.

"Go on up," said the crow. "That's where the bed will be."

Tom held back. The area at the top of the stairs vanished into shadow and Tom could imagine that the witch was waiting there. She had been standing patiently waiting for years perhaps, for another child to capture and fatten in her hen coop, and then cook, and then eat. Tom remembered that in the story the witch had been pushed by little Gretel into the hot oven and burned away into a wisp of smoke. However, in Tom's mind it was perfectly possible that she still lived, and he could easily believe that she was there now, silently waiting in the darkness.

"Go on up, then," said the crow.

"Supposing the witch is up there, waiting?" said Tom.

"Look," said the crow, "she became a puff of smoke, she was all burned up, there is no witch—well, not in this house, anyway."

Tom climbed the stairs carefully, slowly, and the crow hopped up behind him. The candle threw big shadows around the walls as they climbed. Every step higher showed a little more detail of the stairs and the landing at the top. As the darkness dissolved Tom saw that there was no witch waiting for him; there were just the pointy door and the dusty old floor. He opened the bedroom door very slowly. He put his candle hand in through the gap first, then poked his head around the door. No witch, just a pointy-ended bed and torn curtains and a witch's broom in the corner by the pointy bed. The crow perched on the end of the bed and looked as if he were especially carved there to blend in with the room.

Tom settled down to sleep on the musty cover. He felt a lingering edge of real fear. "I'm a bit scared still," he said to Jollity.

"I know, Tom. A sudden creak on the stair outside, a sudden cackle of witch's laughter, something beyond the torn curtains, something cold and clammy touching your face in the dark, that sort of thing?"

"That sort of thing exactly," said Tom with a shiver.

The moonlight shone through the barley-sugar windows, and an owl hooted spookily in the woods outside. Tom thought for a bit and then said to the crow, "Jollity, this is a storybook house, after all, in the Land of Stories."

"It certainly is," said the crow.

"Then it should have an atmosphere of some kind, shouldn't it? It might be a happy atmosphere. It might be a sad atmosphere. It might be a bit of a scary atmosphere, like this one, but whatever it is, it is all part of the story world. And that is your world, and my brothers' world, and my dad's world, and now it's my world, too, and I have to be brave for all of them and for my mum. It is only a story, after all!" He felt comforted and also a bit excited by that.

"Quite right," said the crow. "Good night, Tom."

"Good night, Crow," said Tom.

Tom felt relieved. He had, after all, been brave; only a little bit, maybe, but he had faced up to entering a witch's house. He had faced up to it, and now he felt very snug, even safe, tucked behind the thick raggedy curtains of the witch's pointy bed. His real adventuring life had begun.

CHAPTER 26

Jack's Story
An Interrupted Journey
The Western Lands

J ack set off on his quest in a bad mood. He was the only Trueheart so far in this round of stories to have set off to play the peasant and not the prince. It still annoyed him. Even though his brother Jackson was to suffer transformation into a frog, he was still to be a frog *prince*, and not a frog *peasant*. Jack scuffed at the road with his boots and muttered, "Not fair," under his breath as he walked. His instruction letter had told him to head to the Western Gate. He was to make himself useful at a tumbledown farmhouse that was clearly marked on his map. A farm woman, a poor widow, was to be his mother, and he must help her in any way she chose.

He was not a happy adventurer.

If he was really unlucky, he would no doubt have the same mother as he had had for the Simple Jack story. She was a real old crosspatch who had boxed his ears worse than his own mother ever did. It was enough to try the patience of a saint. The Bureau seemed to have it in for him and no mistake. He passed through the Western Gate, but not before the keeper had made him change, as per Rule 6, into a dingy peasant outfit of very coarse wool, which felt all itchy next to his skin.

By following the map he found the house easily enough. It was very tumbledown and not really much of a farm at all. Jack was sure now that there was little prospect of a good hearty farmhouse supper that night.

When Jack went into the farmyard his heart sank. Sure enough, there she was, the cross, thin-faced woman who had been his mother when he had played Simple Jack.

"Oh, there you are," she said. "Where have you been all day? There's work to be done."

Jack spent an unhappy afternoon doing hard grubby jobs around the farmyard for the cross woman.

They had a miserable supper together of dry rough bread, a hunk of mossy-looking cheese, and a mug of warm water from a cracked cup.

Just before he went to sleep in his mean drafty bedroom, Jack noticed a light in the high window of a mysterious tower near the vegetable garden. Someone must live there, he thought. I wonder who? And with that he fell asleep.

Early the next morning he was sent out to milk the

cow. It was a rather poor-looking cow, very thin, but harmless and perfectly friendly.

"All right, then, old girl," said Jack, who had warmed his hands especially.

"Mwoo," said the cow.

There wasn't much in the way of milk. Jack took the bucket back into the farm stillroom and the cross woman shook her head in disgust.

"We've nothing left, Jack. You must go to market and sell Milky White the cow," she said, "or we shall have nothing to eat, and I mean nothing at all." Jack agreed to go off in the afternoon and do his best.

Jack noticed a beautiful girl looking out of the window of the high tower in the garden. "Who lives up in that there tower, Mother?" he asked.

"As if you don't know, you good-for-nothing scamp. I'll thank you to pay no mind to her and all of that. It does not concern you, as you well know; it's a different story altogether," she whispered. "Any more on that subject and I'll box your ears for you."

Jack let the subject drop, but she was a lovely-looking girl and he couldn't help but be interested in her.

Jack had grown fond of the poor old cow, Milky White. After his meager lunch he set off reluctantly down the road to the fair with her. There was a cattle market at the fair, and Jack was to get the best price he possibly could for the cow.

"It's turning into one of those stories," Jack muttered to himself under his breath as they trudged along. He was feeling like Simple Jack all over again. He had not gone far along the road when a magnificent-looking knight on a white charger appeared, traveling toward

them. As the knight got nearer Jack realized with a sinking heart that it was his own brother Jacquot, who was, of course, playing a very posh prince.

"That's all I need," said Jack to Milky White.

"Moo," said the cow.

Adventurers never ever met each other in the course of their stories. There was, he thought, no actual written rule but he could not remember it happening before, ever. The Story Bureau must be getting sloppy.

"Good morrow, surly peasant," said Jacquot, riding tall in the saddle, and hardly able to contain his laughter.

"Afternoon, *sire*," said Jack with an expression of fury on his face.

"Careful now," said Jacquot. "A little more respect, if you please."

The two men passed each other—Jacquot tall and magnificent in the saddle, his silver armor gleaming in the morning light; Jack, surly and grubby in his itchy drab clothes, pulling the poor old skinny cow along the road with him. After Jacquot had passed, Jack thought about it and decided that it really was a very odd thing indeed—it had never happened before in all his long experience. No adventurer had ever met another one halfway into the other's story. He hoped this wasn't a bad omen. "The lovely girl up in that tower, I'll bet that's where he's off to. Ho ho, he'll get a thick ear from that woman, too, if he tries anything there."

He had not gone much farther down the road when he saw a tall thin man in clerical black clothes. He was walking toward Jack on the other side of the road and appeared agitated.

"Morning," Jack said as they approached each other.

The man stopped and clapped his hand to his forehead. "There you are," he said. "Oh, thank the Master, at last."

"Have you been looking for me, then?" said Jack.

The man crossed the road. He had skin the color of old paper. He looked like someone who spent most of his time either in a very dark and close-shuttered room or under a very damp stone. He shook Jack firmly by the hand and fixed him with a very penetrating gaze. "I have been sent by the Story Bureau," he whispered. "There has been a terrible, terrible mistake."

"I *knew* it," said Jack, gratified.

"You are Jack Trueheart, are you not?" the man whispered again, looking around in case he was being overheard. "Well, I am afraid you have been wrongly . . . designated," he hissed. It seemed to Jack that the air got just a little bit colder every time the man spoke, as if a chill wind suddenly blew in with every word.

"You should have been a prince, the same as your brothers. Everything has been muddled by an idiot at the Bureau. A mistaken letter was sent out."

"Seems very odd," said Jack, and he shook his head. "I've never known the Bureau to make a mistake before. Although I did meet my brother Jacquot, all poshed up in shiny armor on the road a few minutes ago. Never known a thing like *that* to happen before."

"You see, the Master is after all human, fallible," the man said very quietly. "And he isn't getting any younger."

"Yes, but even so," said Jack, "it just seems so unlikely,

what with all the scribes, and the sprites—did no one check?"

"Not until now," said the man. "I checked, and the result is I'm here to stop all this."

"Stop what?" said Jack.

"This particular story, of course," the man replied, and so quietly that Jack found it hard to hear him at all.

He bent his head closer to hear better. He smelled a very sickly sweet smell coming from somewhere. The man in black reached his hand up and quickly smothered Jack's face with a white cloth. Jack felt suddenly as if he would like to go off to sleep straightaway. His legs felt wobbly, and he slumped forward, glad at last for the chance to lie down.

CHAPTER 27

Some Minutes Later at Tumbledown Farm

Jacquot rode past the tumbledown farm, the vegetable plot, and the tall tower. He heard a high fluting voice calling out to him. "Cooee." He looked up and saw a tiny figure waving from a window high in the tower. He rode over, proud and tall in the saddle, his armor gleaming romantically in the sunlight. He knew that he looked every inch the prince, the hero, even though the armor was uncomfortably hot and heavy to wear. When he got nearer to the tower he could see that the waving figure was a very pretty girl with very long flowing hair.

"Are you a prince?" she asked.

"Indeed I am," Jacquot replied, smitten immediately by the beauty of the girl so high above him.

"Have you come to save me?" she called, smiling sweetly at him.

"That's why I'm here," he called back, "that's what I'm for." Jacquot bowed as best he could in the saddle, what with the stiff armor and everything.

"Oh good," she cried, "at last. But there is a problem. There are no stairs up the tower to my chamber. My mama is fierce and likes to keep me up here all to herself."

"That is truly wicked," said Jacquot. "I will set off and scour the kingdom on a special quest to find a way to reach your chamber. Hold tight, my beauty, and I shall soon return and rescue you."

"Oh, thank you, brave prince," she replied. "If I might suggest . . ." and here she whispered. "The bridge that joins the tower to the house, or a simple ladder, might do the trick."

"That would be too easy. I am intended for a brave and princely quest, it should be harder to do than that. Might I inquire the name of the fair maid to whom I am now entirely devoted?"

"Why, my name is Rapunzel. Bless you, my prince, and God speed your return."

Jacquot set off at a gallop. What was needed, he thought, was some way of climbing up to that window. A brave way, that is, a proper story kind of way. Using the skimpy little bridge or a long ladder would be too easy, not heroic enough at all. Find that special, difficult, brave, story way and the prize of the lovely Rapunzel would be his.

He spurred his white charger down the road away from the tumbledown farm and the tower. As he rode he thought how odd it had been passing his brother Jack on the road some way back. But then perhaps Jack might help him to scale the tower. After a while he passed the cow that Jack had had with him. The cow was standing all on its own in a field just off the road, quietly munching at the grass, but there was no sign of Jack, so Jacquot rode on. Farther down the road he saw a man dressed in black standing before a small wood. Jacquot shivered inside his armor at the sight of him, like a ghost in the daylight, and he reigned in his noble horse.

"Excuse me, my good fellow," Jacquot called out to the man, "have you seen a lone peasant on this road? A tall lad, broad, good-looking."

The sinister-looking man stepped away from the tree line. "Dressed in buckram," he said, "a rough tunic, green leggings?"

"Sounds like our Jack, all right," said Jacquot.

"He's just over here," said the man, gesturing to the copse of dark trees behind him.

Jacquot got off his horse and clanked his way over to the man in black. "What, you've seen Jack in these woods here?" he asked.

"Oh yes, come with me," said the man. He led Jacquot in among the trees. It was very quiet in the wood. The trees were planted very closely together, the trunks made a very dense pattern, and the dark overhanging branches all but caused the sky to vanish.

"I saw him just over there," said the man in black. He gestured over to a clearing in the trees. A large basket, as tall as a man, stood in the space. It was covered with ropes and there were small sacks strung around the upper rim. Jacquot walked over to the basket. It puzzled him. What on earth was it for? He stood on tiptoe, the armor clanking as he stretched. He could just see over the rim. Ropes stretched up into the air, tight and springy. He looked up to where they were attached to something huge and round and made of cloth, which hovered above the basket. Now he was even more puzzled. He turned to find the man in black standing quietly right beside him.

"How did you—" Jacquot started to say, but the man in black put his finger to his lips.

"Shhh," he said, and held a large white cloth up in front of Jacquot. The cloth smelled very sweet, like a bunch of roses on a summer afternoon. Jacquot's head swam; he felt faint. He found himself slipping over the edge of the basket, and he landed in a clanking heap at the bottom. He didn't mind, he just felt sleepy, even though it was still daylight. After a moment the basket began to rise. That nice man in black was standing next to him and surely that was Jack slumped in the corner over there. They were in the air now, higher and higher, up beyond the clouds even.

Well, well, thought Jacquot, I am asleep, after all, and plainly dreaming. Jacquot's noble horse whinnied in fear as the balloon rose above the trees, and galloped away as fast as its legs would take it.

CHAPTER 28

On the Road
Some Time Later

Tom and the crow were making good progress on their way through the countryside when they met a cow all on its own. It was happily eating grass in a field by the side of the road.

"Ah, look, a cow," said Tom. "The first one we've seen." The crow settled down near the cow. "Good afternoon, Mrs. Cow," Tom called out cheerily. "Nice day for a walk," he continued. The cow looked up at the crow with her big brown eyes. She kept on chewing. She was a very pale cow. "Have you a name?"

Tom asked, without any hope of a reply.

"I'm to be sold," she said quietly. Tom took a nervous step backward. "It's all right, really," the cow said. "I'm an enchanted cow; I'm part of a story. You are a young Trueheart, unless I miss my guess."

"I am," said Tom.

"My name's Milky White," the cow said wearily.

Tom was surprised that the cow had actually spoken to him, but he managed not to show it. Tom now knew a talking crow and a talking cow; things could get complicated.

The cow lifted her head and looked straight at Tom. "Then Jack would be your older brother," said the cow, her head cocked on one side quizzically.

"Have you seen Jack?" Tom asked amazed.

"He was taking me to the cow market at the fair. We were going along very nicely, minding our own business, when a very sinister man in black came and took him away," said the cow.

"When was this?" Tom asked her.

"I'm not sure," said the cow. "I seem to have been standing in this field just munching for ever such a long time."

"We should take the cow to the fair," said Jollity the crow. "We should continue the story, see it through, see what happens."

"Wait," said Tom, "my brothers have been taken, one after the other—so where does he take them?"

"I can only tell you they went up in the sky," said the cow, and she raised her big brown eyes skyward, "in a strange contraption."

"A contraption," said Tom, "so that's it! Come on, Jollity, we'll walk to the fair as you suggested. We'll find out what's going on, and Milky White the cow is coming with us."

With that the crow flew up and circled above them.

"Right," said Tom, "come on, nice old Milky White, we are just going for a little walk."

He stepped in front of the cow, found the rope, took up the slack, and gave a tug to it. As it tightened the cow let out a very cowlike "Mwooo," and trotted forward. Its wet nose bumped against Tom's nose, and for a long minute they stared into each other's eyes, nose to nose. Then the cow gave Tom's face a very friendly lick.

"Ugh," Tom said.

"Pleased to meet you," said the cow.

Tom draped his winter cloak across the cow's back. "Nice Milky White," he kept saying, "nice cow." It seemed a very large animal to Tom, but it did have a friendly face, he had to admit.

Tom had never been to a fair, but his older brothers had often talked about them. They were more fun than just the usual market and full of people and noise and music. His brothers had talked about the men who worked at the fairgrounds. They said that some of these men couldn't be trusted, that there were such people as card-sharps. Tom had never realized that cards needed sharp-ening, and he had pictured in his head a man dressed in a dark cloak, his face in shadow, working away at the edges of a playing card with a glinting sharp knife. They also said that there were pickpockets, and tricksters of all kinds, and that at the fair you had to keep your wits about you. Tom may not have known what a cardsharp was, but he had a good idea of what a trickster might be, and he knew he must be careful of them. He was somehow sure he would be very easily tricked, what with being so young.

It was a warm afternoon, and it was very pleasant to stroll along the road in the sunshine, surrounded by all the spring flowers. As long as he didn't think too much about sinister men and flying contraptions, Tom could see that a life on the road, adventuring like this, was fun. They heard the fair long before they could see it. The distant sound of jolly piping organ music came drifting down the road. Tom patted Milky White on her flank now and then and encouraged her along the road.

"Come on, old girl," he said. "And by the way, once we are at the fair, no more talking."

"Understood," said Milky White.

CHAPTER 29

At the Fairground

There was the strong smell of frying onions and presently, in nearby fields, Tom saw the fair. There were gaily striped tents, in blue, yellow, and red. There were banners fluttering in the afternoon light. They could hear jolly music from the fairground organ. There were crowds of jolly people, with jolly children dancing around a jolly maypole, jolly sideshows, a jolly old carnival slide, a hall of mirrors, and all sorts of jolly fun. The crow flew off to find the market tent while Tom enjoyed himself drifting from attraction to attraction with the cow.

The crow flew back and settled on Tom's shoulder. "I found the cattle market," said the crow quietly. "It's in a tent at the other end of the fair."

Milky White pawed the ground and hung her head.

"What's up, Milky White?" said Tom.

The sad cow looked up at him and whispered, "When you've sold me, take the money back to Tumbledown Farm. It's on the map. You do have a map?"

"Yes I do," said Tom.

"Remember, Tumbledown Farm, that's where Jack would have gone," and the cow winked at him.

"Right," said Tom, "no more talking."

They found the cattle market tent; the flap was closed and tied with a rope. An envelope was attached by sprite ribbon to the rope. The envelope was addressed to *Jack Trueheart, Esquire.* Tom opened the envelope and pulled out the parchment letter.

Take the offer from the man in green.
Whatever he offers you must accept.
The Story Bureau

Tom pocketed the letter. "I will do exactly what Jack would have done," he said. The crow waited outside while Tom took Milky White into the tent. The floor was covered with straw and a group of men stood around the edges. They were all dressed as farmers. As soon as Tom and the cow came through the entrance, the men all suddenly sprang to life. It was as if the farmers had been simply waiting for Tom and the cow to appear. They gathered around and began appraising Milky White. They looked her over, prodded her about, and muttered complimentary things.

"A fine animal," said one.

"Never seen a finer," said another.

"Worth a whole bag of gold," said yet another, patting her flank.

The cow looked from one to the other and shook her head. One farmer held out a heavy linen bag, which jingled. "Would this be enough?" he asked. "There's a whole hundred gold sovereigns in here."

The cow mooed.

"I'll give you two hundred," said a red-faced man with a straw in his mouth and polished leather gaiters on his legs.

"Make it three hundred," said yet another, "and that's my final offer." So much money for one cow; it didn't seem possible or likely.

Another man stepped forward. He was wearing a green coat, trousers the color of meadow grass in April, and a tall green stovepipe hat. He had a friendly red face and smiled at Tom.

"I'll offer these," he said very quietly, and he held his hand out.

Tom looked down and saw an unwrapped twist of green paper and five dull brown beans.

"Beans," Tom said. "They're not worth much, are they?"

"Oh," said the man, "but these are *special* beans."

The farmers all laughed.

"They would have to be *very* special," one of them said.

"These *are* very special," whispered the man in green. "These are *magic* beans."

"Magic?" Tom said loudly in surprise.

"Shhh, yes, magic," said the man.

The farmers all laughed again, and Milky White let out a long low "Moo."

The man with the bag of sovereigns jingled them under Tom's nose. "Final offer," he said. "Take it or leave it."

The man in green . . . "I'll take . . . the beans," Tom said.

There was uproar in the tent; the farmers could hardly control their laughter. "You'll get in trouble, my lad," one of them said.

The man in green took the rope from Tom and gently stroked Milky White about the ears. "There, there," he said, and he handed the packet of beans over to Tom. "Plant these only at night when there's a moon showing, and you shall see real magic. They are worth more than any gold sovereigns," he said, and he raised his hat with a wink.

Tom put the little twist of paper with the beans in his pocket. Then he patted Milky White on the flank.

"Bye-bye, old Milky White," he said. "I'll miss you." He had grown quite fond of that gentle animal.

"Bye, Tom," the cow whispered back, and then winked at him.

The man in green handed Tom the winter cloak, and then he gently led the cow out of the tent. Tom followed them. The cow looked back and gave Tom a sad farewell moo.

"Remember," the man in green said, "you must plant the beans only at night." And then he went off with Milky White following slowly behind him.

The crow flew down from the tent. "I hope you got a good price."

"Well, of course I did," said Tom. They went back to the gate, ignoring all the fun and gaiety of the fair. It was late afternoon and near sunset. "We must find Tumbledown Farm before it's too dark to see," said Tom. "Milky White told me that was what we must do with the money I got for her. They're sure to know what to do when we get there." Tom pulled the Land of Stories map out of his traveling bag. Tumbledown Farm was marked some way down the road.

Tom was sad to leave the lights and music of the fair but it was time to go. He walked up the long road toward the setting sun. He went up the hills and down them again. Around and around he went, and then he came into a deeply wooded area where owls were hooting. The crow bobbed along happily on Tom's shoulder. Tom was not so happy; it was getting really dark now. He couldn't help thinking of the kind of things that lay in wait for unwary travelers. How many times had his brothers come back from a story where they had encountered a fierce wolf or something worse on a woodland path. It was all very well hearing about such adventures while settled around the cozy fireside at home, quite another to remember them in the middle of a dark wood as he was now. He touched the dwarf sword, safe on his belt, and felt better. He pulled it out and the blade shone like silver, reflecting what little light there was and acting almost like a beacon through the darkening wood around them.

Tom thought about the magic beans. He stopped and took out the twist of paper from his tunic. He unwrapped it and looked down at the little drab beans—could they really be magic?

The crow came and looked at them, too. "What are those?" he asked.

"These are magic beans. I sold the cow for them," Tom said.

"No money, then," the crow said.

"No," said Tom.

"Uh-oh, I see," said the crow.

"I'm only going to hand over four of them. I'll keep one back. If they are magic then it might come in very useful," said Tom.

"I can't comment," said the crow and flew off with a "caw" sound.

Eventually they arrived at Tumbledown Farm. It was totally dark now, and in the clouded moonlight Tom couldn't see very much of the building itself. He noticed that the shutters were hanging off the windows, and he saw that there was a high rickety wooden bridge that led from the attic of the farmhouse to a tall tower that stood in the garden nearby. The crow flew up and settled on the porch. Tom knocked on the door and he was suddenly pulled roughly into a dark kitchen. The crow flew down and perched outside the window and peered in.

"Well, then," said a voice, "where on earth have you been? It's about time you were back—hand it over." Tom was face-to-face with a thin-faced and very cross-looking woman. "Something's happened to you since you left to sell that miserable cow; you look half the size that you did before. Still, never ask for reasons in this barmy place, I always say. Never mind the no-apology for being late, either, just give me the money."

Tom nervously handed over the little paper twist with the dull brown beans carefully wrapped in it.

"Not very heavy," she said, weighing the little green

package in her hand. She put it on the table, and with the tip of her tongue poking out between her thin lips in concentration, she very slowly and very carefully unwrapped the twist of paper. She looked down at the little pile of beans. She waited a moment, and then she looked over at Tom. She quickly looked under the table. Then she dragged a kitchen chair out, which made a horrible squealing noise on the stone floor. She lifted up the chair, bent down, and looked under it. Then she looked at Tom again. "Where's the money? This had better be one of your silly jokes, Jack," she said, and rolled up the sleeves of her ragged dress. "That cow was worth *something*, at least, not *nothing at all*. These look like nothing to me; they look like the contents of your head, nothing, empty. No wonder they all call you Simple Jack." She shook her head. "You'll be the death of me, Jack."

Tom looked out at the darkness beyond the window, at the unknown and frightening world pressing in all around him, where his only friend left was a talking crow. He knew that he had to play along and just be Jack for now.

"I sent you out ages ago in good faith to sell that useless skinny cow for some money to buy food, and you've come back with these pathetic . . . things. WHAT ARE THEY?"

"Beans," he said.

"BEANS!" she screamed. "Beans," she whispered, "one, two, three, four little beans. Someone offered you these pathetic beans for our cow, and you took them, Jack. What do we do with them now, *EAT* THEM?"

"No," Tom said quietly.

She tiptoed around the table and stood over him. "No?" she said.

"No," he said. He was actually quaking with fear, and it was an effort to stop himself from crying like a big baby. He would feel like such a fool crying in front of her. "The man said I should plant them, in the garden, in the dark, by moonlight. You see . . . they're . . . they're . . . magic beans."

"Oh, *magic beans*," she whispered. She changed her expression suddenly, and a creepy grin appeared on her face, showing her big teeth. "I see, well, that's different, isn't it? You should have said so before. Look, Jack *dearest*, there's such a lovely new moon up now, I can see it through the window." She scuttled over to the window and flung it open, causing the crow to fly off in a flap. "So, I think I'll just quickly, but oh so very carefully, plant these lovely, 'magic' beans that you so *cleverly* swapped for our only cow, in our garden, in the . . . DARK." And with that she hurled the four beans out, high into the night air, and then slammed the window shut again.

"Well, Jack, that's that; we should have a good crop of plain dull beans to eat in, oh, a few weeks, and that will feed us all very well . . . WON'T IT," she shouted, right in his face. Then she gave his ear a twist and pushed him out of the room. He bit his lip, trying his best not to show this woman how upset he was.

"Now," she said, "it's up to bed for you, with no supper, of course, and on your way up those stairs, do not, I repeat, *not*, disturb anyone."

He began to climb the stairs. They were much more frightening than the stairs at home. The stairs went on and on. All was total darkness. The stair treads were high, so he had to stretch his legs up each time and hold on to the banister rail as he went. There were noises, too, not the friendly teasing laughter of his brothers at home, but a sinister fluttering and skittering from the darkness. The house was old and decrepit, so that there might have been bats or, much worse, ghosts living in it. It certainly looked haunted. The woman stood at the bottom of the stairs and watched him as he climbed up, every step of the way.

"Not a peep out of you till the morning," she said.

He reached a landing at the top of the stairs. A corridor stretched ahead of him. He could just make out a series of doors, and a window at the far end. Then he heard a tapping noise. It sounded like something sharp scraping across a pane of glass. A twig, perhaps, was blowing against the window, or, he thought, worse, the hand of a skeleton was tapping to be let in. He had always been very scared of skeletons.

There were two doors. While he was choosing which one he should open, the nearest door began to open very slowly all on its own. He watched, frozen with horror, as a faint light spilled into the hallway and something frightening moved out from behind the door, a pale shape, a shadow that floated against the darkness. It came toward him on a gust of wind.

His worst fear had finally come true, and a ghost skeleton was coming to get him. He was in a ghost story, not an adventure story after all. He closed his eyes and braced himself against the wall: he couldn't move. He was aware of his heart pounding like a drum in his chest. However, something deep down inside him, some hidden reserve, some little spark of the adventuring instinct, of which he was quite unaware, forced his arm to move down to his belt and very slowly and quietly pull out the sword. He held it straight in front of him. The sword shook almost as much as he did himself.

"Oh, there you are at last. Welcome again, my prince," came a lightly whispered sweet voice. He opened his eyes. The most beautiful girl he had ever seen was standing in front of him. She was impossibly beautiful. She had thick dark blonde hair and large clear eyes the color of the sea; her dress was long and white with a pattern of little birds all over it. She leaned forward like a vision and offered him her cheek for a kiss.

"I'm sorry, miss," he said. "I'm not your prince."

"Shhh, speak quietly or she will hear us. Of course you are my prince," she whispered. "Now, come on, up off your knees, and we will finally escape together."

"I'm not on my knees," he whispered. "I'm standing up."

The girl came a little closer. "Oh dear," she said, "so you are. Well, if you're not my prince returned, then who are you?"

"I'm Tom Trueheart," he said, "apprentice Boy Adventurer."

The girl quickly pulled him after her and clicked the door shut quietly behind her. Tom found himself standing with the lovely girl on the rickety bridge. She took his hand and led him along the broken walkway and through a little door in the side of the tower. He found himself in a round room, and in the sudden lamplight he noticed that the girl's hair was very, very long. It tumbled down in waves from her head and snaked about the room in great golden coils. He could even see her hair trailing under the bedside table, around the legs of the bed itself, and across the worn-looking rag rug, where it finally twisted itself around the mirror and washstand. Her long hair trailed everywhere.

"I was expecting my prince to come back, you see," she said. "He said he would. He had to go away; he had to work out a way of getting in here by climbing the high tower. She never lets me out."

"She's very fierce," said Tom.

"He wore bright armor and had a sword. He was very handsome."

"Sounds like Jacquot to me," said Tom. "You see, I've got six brothers and they are all called Jack. There's Jack, Jacquot, Jackson, Jacques, Jake, and Jackie; they're the ones who have all the adventures. I haven't even begun my training yet."

"It was one of your brothers, then, that was meant to come back here and rescue me," said the beautiful girl. "He was going to work out a special way to climb all the way up to my window and then whisk me away for a life of romance. She can control the entrance to that dangerous little bridge we just crossed. Oh, I wonder what can have happened to him?"

She held out her slim elegant hand to Tom. "I'm so sorry, I haven't introduced myself. My name is Rapunzel," she added, with a polite curtsy.

"I'm looking for my brothers, my lady. One by one they have vanished halfway through their stories. I was looking for my brother Jack when I found a talking cow. I had to sell the cow to a man in green who gave me five beans, only he said they were magic beans. And that woman, your mother, I think," and here Tom paused, "said she was *my* mother, and she pulled my ear and tried to make me cry, only she isn't my mother, really. My mother's at home waiting for me and all my older brothers to come home safely. They do all the adventuring normally, not me. When I had sold the cow, I brought the beans back here. That woman is so cross because I swapped the cow for the beans and the man in green said you had to plant the magic beans at night when there was a moon, so then the woman threw the magic beans out of the window, except one that I kept in case. Then there is my friend Jollity the crow, who is a bird and can talk as well as fly." He stopped suddenly and drew a very long deep breath.

"Goodness, it sounds like you're having quite an adventure already," said the beautiful girl.

Jollity the crow, fed up with tapping his beak on the landing window and getting no response from Tom, flew around the outside of Tumbledown Farmhouse. He landed on the ledge of first one window and then another, looking for Tom. The first room he looked in was dark and gloomy, and the crow could see the frightening woman, the one who played Jack's mother. She was fast asleep and snoring in her bed. The crow certainly didn't want to risk waking her. He flew over to the tall tower and landed on the one high window ledge. He peeped in on a room lit with dim yellow lantern light. Tom was in the room talking to a young woman in a long dress. The crow tapped on the window with his beak. Tom heard what he thought were the skeleton fingers, tap-tapping again, only they were much nearer now.

"Shhh," he said, "can you hear that?"

Rapunzel fell silent and they both listened. A tap, tap, tap came from the turret window. Tom looked over and saw the crow outside on the ledge.

"Oh," he said with relief, "so that's who was tapping at

the window. It's just my friend the crow, not a skeleton after all."

Tom opened the window, and the crow hopped in. As Tom pulled the window shut he heard an enormous noise and felt a rush of air from the garden below. It was a rustling, and a crackling, and a stretching, as if something very big was growing just below the window. Then something huge came blundering and thundering up through the bushes very fast in the dark. Something very big had just gone up high into the sky.

"What was that?" he said.

"I felt it, too," said the crow.

"Ooh, he really does talk," said Rapunzel. "He's very sweet."

She stroked the crow's shiny black-feathered head. Jollity the crow suffered the stroking quite happily, tilting his head on one side. "I have been in despair, you know." She sat down in front of her looking glass and brushed at her lovely heavy blonde hair. "I was so fed up this evening, so miserable, before you came, that I was going to cut off all my long hair just to annoy that cross woman."

She picked up a pair of big shiny scissors from her dressing table. "It would be so easy, you see, just chop it all across here and I would have a nice sensible bob.

"Perhaps I should do it anyway; do you think it would suit me?"

She picked up a great chunk of her hair, and Tom finally saw just how much of it there was. It really was the longest and most beautiful hair he had ever seen. It must have been at least long enough to reach all the way down to the ground from the tower window.

"You don't answer," she said. "No one much cares what happens to me. My prince has gone away and may never come back. I am stuck up here all day on my own. Oh well, here goes nothing." She roughly grabbed a chunk of her lovely hair and held the scissors up to her jawline.

"No, wait," said Tom, "don't do that. I think your hair is really pretty; it suits you. Besides, it's given me an idea about how my brother might rescue you, so please don't cut it all off, Miss Rapunzel."

"I agree," said the crow, nodding his beak.

"Well," she said, hesitating, "if you are both sure."

"Oh yes," said Tom.

"Definitely," said the crow.

Rapunzel put down the scissors. She stretched her arms wide and yawned. "It's late and we should all get some sleep," she said. "Let's try and meet in the morning. Remember, hope makes a bad supper but a good breakfast. Something tells me that we will be good friends, my sweet little adventurer." She patted Tom on the head.

"You, too, Mr. Crow." The crow dipped his head, and Rapunzel gave him a quick tickle under the beak.

"I hope you find your brother soon. I think you two will arrange my rescue yet. Good night, then, and go very quietly."

"Good night, miss," Tom whispered, and once she wasn't looking he picked up the shiny scissors and slipped them into his satchel.

"Good night," said the crow.

They crept back along the little bridge and went into a dark bedroom in the farmhouse attic. It was deathly cold in the room so Tom huddled into his cloak for warmth. There were two beds. "I'll take the big bed," said the crow yawning.

Tom was far too tired to argue with the crow about birds and nests, and people and beds, and he soon fell into a deep sleep, hungry and exhausted, in the smaller bed.

CHAPTER 30

Tumbledown Farm, 7:00 A.M.

The next thing he knew it was early morning, and he was being shaken rudely awake.

"Well, you've really gone and done it this time, Jack."

"What?" he said, sitting up in the tiny bed.

He was pulled up by the ear and his nose was squashed hard against the window.

"That's what," said the shrill woman.

Tom was confused. He could see bright green leaves outside the window, and he could see some blue sky and a few fluffy clouds—all in all it looked like a very nice morning. He wriggled his ear free. "I don't know what you mean," he said.

"Look again," she said, and she kept his poor face pressed up close against the glass. Then Tom saw it.

It was very tall and it was very green. It had four stalks, each as thick as a good-sized oak tree, all twisted together, and it was growing right outside the window. When he looked up he could see that it stretched up higher than the tower, straight on up into the sky until it vanished into the blue.

"So much for your magic beans," she said, and fetched him a stinging clout on the head. "Look at my poor garden, all my best green plants and vegetables ruined."

She allowed him time to pull on his stout boots and then she pushed him out of the door and down the stairs. She dragged him outside into the garden. There the strange thundering and rushing and rustling noises of the night before were explained. Where the magic beans had been thrown out of the window and scattered, a huge, massive, enormous, giant beanstalk had forced itself out of the ground during the night.

It had pushed up great mounds and lumps of dark earth and pebbles and soil and strange-looking vegetables and scattered them all over the garden. Now it stretched up into the sky much higher and farther than Tom could see. Only by craning his neck right back could he see the very tip of the stalk as it disappeared way beyond the clouds.

The crow was sitting on one of the lower leaves of the beanstalk and he nodded his head in the direction of an envelope that was tied around one of the leaf stems.

The woman went into the house and came back straightaway with an axe. "Well, you can chop those awful great tree things down right now; it's the least you can do for me," she said. "We can make a lovely bitter green soup out of the stalks and leaves. That'll last us nicely for many, many meals. And make sure you chop it down carefully so that it doesn't fall anywhere near the house."

Tom looked up and saw that the lovely Rapunzel was peeping at them out of her open window. "So *that's* what that noise was in the night," Rapunzel said prettily. "Now, Mother, you see what magic can do."

"Rapunzel, my girl, you get inside and you stay inside," the woman shouted.

Rapunzel closed her window, but she waved a last friendly wave to Tom from behind the glass.

Tom pretended to chop away at the base of the beanstalk but he did it very feebly. The woman went back into the house and slammed her tumbledown door shut. After a minute or two he put the axe down and stretched up for the envelope. He couldn't quite reach, being so small, so he climbed up a bit among the lower leaves until he could. The envelope was addressed to *Jack Trueheart, Esquire.* Tom tore it open anyway. The letter said:

Climb up the Beanstalk and never stop.
Keep on going right up until you reach the top.

"Jack was going to have to climb this thing, all the way up," Tom said to the crow, and he looked up again into the distant blue sky. He was terrified of heights. It was one thing to stand on the giant leaves of the beanstalk's lower branches—you could jump off so easily and land safely on the ground on your own two feet—but quite another to think of climbing up beyond the clouds.

"I can't do it," he said.

"You must do it," said the crow, "or the story won't work out."

"What story?" Tom said.

"Jack's story, of course," said the crow. "This is the next part of our adventure."

"I have an adventure down here already on the ground. Rapunzel expects me to arrange her rescue from that woman," Tom said.

"I thought she said she was expecting your brother the prince to rescue her. If so, then that's the prince's adventure, not yours."

"I would like to rescue her, though; she's so nice," said Tom.

"You are to rescue your *brothers*, remember."

"I know," said Tom.

"One of your brothers will rescue her, and the other brothers will rescue all the others that they are supposed to rescue. You have your own adventure now: you have to help them to finish their stories. That is your mission, clear and simple. We have to follow the clues whatever they may be, and see where they lead. The letter says to climb this beanstalk, and so we had better get on with it. Come on, I'll fly up with you, but we'd better hurry up before that woman comes out again."

"I don't like being up high, though," Tom said. "I'm frightened of falling."

"The trick is not to look down," said the crow. "Come on, you'll be fine."

CHAPTER 31

Some Way Up the Beanstalk

The crow kept Tom company, flying near him, but hopping mostly from leaf to leaf, while Tom climbed beside him up the giant beanstalk. At first it was a steady enough climb. The leaves were evenly spaced around the wide stem and all he had to do was hang on to the ones above his head and climb around the stem, treading onto higher leaves with each turn. The leaves were broad and firm and regularly spaced and seemed to support his weight easily. He was still very frightened, though; after all, the higher he went the farther he had to fall.

He kept his face looking in toward the stem as he climbed as the crow had told him not to look down, and he did his very best not to. He did look up from time to time, and the effect of that was almost as bad as he imagined looking down might be. The stem of the beanstalk seemed to sway or even to topple over toward him as he looked up at it. He could feel himself, at various points on the climb, wanting to suddenly give up, let go, and fall backward, to float slowly back down to the ground. The sensible part of him knew that he wouldn't really float down to the ground, but instead would fall very, very fast until he would be brought to a full stop on the ground, with a bone-breaking crash.

"Don't think about it," he told himself. After a while they were far too high to even consider turning back. He looked up and saw a ragged edge of fluffy whiteness. He had nearly reached the clouds.

At that moment, for the first time, he finally couldn't resist looking down. It was a big mistake.

The beanstalk snaked away from below his boots. It

seemed to go on down for miles and miles, until it ended as a tiny line of green near what looked to him like a very tiny toy house. He could see the stem moving, and the leaves rippling in the wind. The beanstalk cast a long, long shadow over the hills, and then far away, to the horizon.

Tom suddenly felt giddy and the world began to spin. He could feel his boots slipping on the wet leaves, his suddenly wet hands were losing their grip on the leaf stems above his head, and he was sure he was going to fall, all the way down to the ground.

The crow said, "We're doing very well, Tom, just the clouds to get through then we'll see what's what above them."

Tom couldn't reply, he was hypnotized by the miniature spinning world far away below him.

"Are you all right, Tom?" said Jollity. "Oh no, no, you've looked down at the ground, haven't you?" The crow could see from Tom's frozen fearful expression that that was exactly what he had done and that he might fall at any second; he could see his hands already slipping, letting go of the leaves.

"Look at me, Tom," said the crow. "Come on now, just look at me, never mind what's going on down there, concentrate on me and you'll be fine." The crow flew close and hovered by Tom's face. Momentarily distracted by the sudden breeze from the crow's wings, Tom looked upward.

"That's it," said the crow, "now you're doing it, that's the way, come on now, just look at me. We're going upward, not downward—never look down. I said the other morning all that time ago that you would need courage, do you remember? You really need it now, Tom. Be brave, first move one foot, then the other, come on."

By keeping his eyes fixed on the crow, Tom just managed to pull himself up. He dared to let go of the leaf stems, and for a split second his hands were free, and he was balancing by just his slippery boots. He could so easily have fallen off backward. But he didn't; he reached up to a higher stem and held on tight. He grabbed first one, and then the next, and so on, and so on, until gradually he found himself higher up, and firmly inside the strange milky light of the clouds, where there was no view of the ground to distract him.

He rested for a moment with his face against the trunk. He felt weak; he was trembling all over and breathing hard.

"Thank you, Jollity, you saved me," he said finally.

"No, no," said the crow, "you saved yourself, Tom. You're the one who had to dare to reach up for those higher branches, and you did it. You showed real courage, and that had to come from inside you. I couldn't make you do it. I think, Thomas Trueheart, that you're on your way to becoming a real adventurer."

After a brief rest among the upper leaves, Tom climbed higher still, until suddenly he cleared the soft cloud shapes that were all around him, and emerged into another world.

Part Three

The End

CHAPTER 32

The World Above the Clouds

Tom and the crow found themselves looking at a whole new landscape. The world above the clouds.

Where the clouds faded off, they edged and fringed the landscape with a heavy mist. Hills and valleys and tall trees stuck up out of the cloud tops. It looked to Tom a little like an autumn morning back in his home forest. A winding road stretched and curled in front of him, looping over and around the hills, and twisting some way away to a tall dark castle on a far hilltop.

The crow flew off the beanstalk and landed on the

road. "It feels quite solid," he said, "come on."

Tom closed his eyes, counted to three, and jumped from the top of the beanstalk. It felt just like leaping onto his bed at home. As Tom leaped he hoped that there was nothing hiding there deep under the mist.

Tom landed safely on the road and looked around. The colors of this new "Sky Land" were very different from those of the land below the beanstalk. The trees, which stuck up across the landscape like so many lollipops, had pink leaves instead of green. The whole effect was a strange unnatural brightness of color everywhere. The very rounded small hills were all picked out in different candy colors: orange, pale green, blue, and a similar sugary pink to the leaves. It looked as if everything around him was made out of sweets. Tom decided that he should head for the castle. The road ahead of him led in just one direction. Looking at the colors of this world above the clouds, and thinking of candy, made him realize just how hungry he was.

"I'm starving," he said to the crow. "I've had nothing to eat since the gingerbread picnic."

"I'll see if I can find some fruit trees or something else for us to eat. You go and explore on foot," said the crow, and he flew off, leaving Tom all on his own.

Tom walked down the road toward the castle. The sky above was a bright blue, but it was as cold as a winter morning back at home, there was such a chill in the air, and Tom was glad of his bulky winter cloak. Off to one side of the road there was a whole forest of the pink-leaved trees. Rough twisted paths led through and around the trunks. Tom, however, kept to the road. There was such a sense of otherness and a darkness deep among those strange bright trees, that he decided to keep away from them. The road to the castle snaked away in front of him, and as he walked he kept his eyes open for any other Story Bureau envelopes or clues. There had been nothing since he reached the top of the beanstalk.

The castle loomed on the hilltop, and got even bigger, the nearer Tom came. The hill that the castle stood on was not the same bright candy color as the rest of the landscape. It was granite gray, with mottled brown patches all over it. There were trees scattered on the slopes leading to the castle, but these trees were bare, without any candy leaves on them, and the naked branches were white and tangled together like skeleton fingers. The castle itself was gray and solid and huge, casting a wide shadow across the road. As Tom drew nearer he could see that it was also a ruin in places: one of the towers leaned at an angle and was supported by wooden beams tied with rope hawsers like the mast of a ship. Tom was nervous, both of what he would find at the castle and of the surrounding landscape that he passed, at once so bright and cheerful and also dark and coldly mysterious. The road ahead curled around some of the smaller hills, and was sometimes lost to sight. Tom followed all the turns in the road rather than risk taking any shortcuts over the candy hills. Around one of the bends he came across an unexpected sight.

CHAPTER 33

A Meeting on the Road

A tall thin man in black clothes was also walking along the road. Tom hadn't expected to see anyone before he reached the castle. He looked around for his friend Jollity the crow, but there was no sign of him.

Tom was soon near enough to the walking man for him to hear the sound of Tom's boots. He swiveled his narrow head and looked back down the road at Tom.

"Good morning, sir," Tom said.

The man turned, clearly puzzled. Ormestone saw at once that Tom was dressed as a shrimp-sized version of those awful Trueheart adventurers. While he waited for Tom to catch up with him, he thought fast. He had not counted on having to bother with a younger brother, but now that the creature was so nearly in his grasp, why not get rid of him as well.

"How nice to meet such a polite child in these troubled times," said the man. "Tell me, lad, how did you manage to find yourself all the way up here? I felt sure that I was one of the only travelers who even knew of this place."

"That's a long story," said Tom.

"Well now," said the thin man, "we are fellow travelers, and you are a hungry one, I'll be bound. Would you care to join me in my little picnic? There's plenty for both of us, and then you can tell me all about yourself." The man seemed friendly enough, although Tom did feel that it had gotten even colder since he had met him.

"I am hungry, sir, it's true," said Tom.

"Then we are well met," said the man, and he gestured

to a spot under a tree just off the road. The man opened his basket and took out a cloth and then some bundles and packages, a plate or two, and some bottles. He arranged some dainty sandwiches on a plate and offered one to Tom.

Tom put down his packstaff and sat on the grass.

"Cheese and tomato," said the man in a very soft voice like a whisper, "moist and slightly squished, I'm afraid." The word "squished" sounded especially scary to Tom, but he was too hungry to care much. He took one of the little sandwiches.

"Take two, they're very small," said the man. "Would you like a drink? I have beer, or I have lemonade. I suspect the lemonade for you, the other is perhaps more suitable for an older gentleman such as myself. You look to be about ten years old, would I be right?"

"I'm twelve, actually, sir," Tom said. "My birthday was just the other day."

"Twelve," said the man. "Well, well. Ah me, to be twelve again, with the whole of life ahead of you. Where are you off to, may I ask? You said it was a long story; do tell me."

"I am making for the castle," said Tom, and here he hesitated. How much should he say about himself? He supposed it was obvious to anyone that he was an adventurer of some sort, by his clothes and his packstaff. He had been warned by the Master, after all, to be very wary.

"Ah yes, the castle," said the man. "Very big, isn't it?"

"Why yes, it is," said Tom.

"I am heading in the direction of the castle myself. We could walk there together perhaps. It is always pleasant to walk with a companion. How did you get all the way up here?" asked the man. "An exciting balloon ascent, perhaps, or some newer kind of flying contraption?"

"No, I climbed a giant *beanstalk*," said Tom, who then immediately wished he hadn't said anything of the sort. But it was too late now—he really had to be more careful.

"Your story gets more and more interesting," said the man. "A giant *beanstalk*, you say. Did you just discover this giant beanstalk as you were out walking?"

"Yes," said Tom.

The man turned to Tom with a smile on his face. "I think you are some kind of adventurer," he said as he looked Tom up and down: Tom's cloak, the round shield across one shoulder, the staff and bundle.

"Oh, you mean all this," said Tom. "No, I found the stuff by the road on my walk."

"Oh, you found it? I see, very well," said the man, looking right through Tom with his penetrating steely eyes.

When they had finished, the man carefully cleared away the picnic things. As Tom watched him he caught sight of something: it was a piece of the special Trueheart bundle cloth. The man quickly covered it up, but not before Tom had seen it, and Tom understood in an instant what that glimpse must mean. He now had a very good reason not to like this man. He had every reason to fear him, to hate him above all things.

"I think I'll just carry on exploring on the road now, then," said Tom. "Thank you for the sandwiches, sir. I won't bother with the castle after all perhaps; it looks a bit gloomy and boring."

"You were most welcome to the sandwiches," the man replied. "I would be very careful how you go, there may be all sorts of *dangers* around here," he whispered.

"I'm sure there are," said Tom, looking directly back into the man's pale eyes. Tom had no clue really what to do. There was no sign of Jollity the crow, either. He set off walking, and he could feel the cold-eyed gaze of the man burning into his back. He turned a bend in the road and then as soon as he was out of sight he simply ran as fast as he could. He was very fast, too, his young legs pumping hard as he ran flat out toward the sinister castle. He didn't dare turn to look back at the road behind him. He knew that the terrible man in black would be there right behind him. He reached the castle out of breath but some way ahead of the man. He scanned the road behind and the trees around for the crow, but there was no sign of him anywhere. Tom was seriously worried now. He had no choice but to go up and into the castle to hide; he felt sure that the castle would hold a clue as to what had happened to his brothers. Perhaps they were all locked away somewhere inside. If so it was up to him to find them and rescue them.

There were very steep steps up to the castle, which looked almost impossibly high, looming over him. The black-and-white skull-and-crossbones flag flapped and cracked in the cold wind; it was a seriously desolate place.

Tom started with the first step. It was huge, much bigger than a step really needed to be. He had to use all the little crags and bumps and fissures in the surface of the stone as climbing points. When he finally reached the top, he found himself breathless, looking up at the huge wooden door of the castle.

The door was made of massive knotty planks. There was a huge doorknocker, far too high up the door for anyone of Tom's size to be able to reach it, even by holding his packstaff as high as he could. The lower edge of the door, however, was chipped and sections of it were fully gouged out and the ends of some of the planks were split and worn so that great triangular holes had been left below the iron strap supports. After looking up at the knocker hopelessly, Tom realized that with a bit of squeezing it might be possible to get into the castle through one of these holes. Like a little mouse, he thought. As he pushed his shoulder and arm into the gap he spotted the man in black almost at the steps. The hole was just wide enough, almost as if it had been made for the purpose, and Tom was able to pull himself through the hole into the hallway of the castle.

CHAPTER 34

What Happened to the Crow

Jollity didn't much care for the atmosphere of this world above the clouds. He flew over it looking at the strange colors, the cold light, the gloomy-looking huge castle on the horizon. He had heard from Cicero during his training about the other lands associated with the Land of Stories, the Island of Dark Stories, for instance, and this place had more in common with how he imagined that to be, chilling and scary and unsettling. He flew low looking for any orchards or useful crops or even water supplies. He saw a field of plants that were all

covered over with bright red fruit. He flew down, and he could smell the sweet fruity smell. Strawberries, delicious, just right, he thought. Tom will be pleased. The strawberry plants were lined across the field not far from the snaking road. He could easily lead Tom there. He couldn't resist tasting one. He dived down to ground level and swooped toward the line of plants. Something hooked his feet, and he flapped his wings uselessly as he fell into the nets draped all over the strawberries. He was caught up in the fine netting and could hardly move.

CHAPTER 35

Inside the Castle

Tom stood for a moment and allowed his eyes to grow accustomed to the gloom. He found himself in a very high room where the walls vanished into deep darkness high above him. He could just make out another door on the other side of the hall. It was half open, and a beam of light spilled out around it and across the floor. He walked toward the door, slowly, carefully, and quietly. It was like stepping through a strange landscape just crossing the vast hallway. When he was near enough to the door gap he stopped, craned forward, and peeped into the next room.

He saw huge pieces of furniture. The biggest and most massive chairs he had ever seen, grouped around a long, tall, crudely made table. There was a square wooden cage on the table, and odd lengths of thick rope spilled down on one side.

There came a noise like thunder and the floor shook beneath Tom's feet. The plates and crockery chimed and jingled on the huge table. The thunderous noise came in regular beats, as if a huge creature were coming toward him down the corridor. *Boom, boom, boom, boom*, louder and louder, nearer and nearer. *Stamp . . . stamp . . .* Tom crouched as low as he could, buried his head in his hands, and made himself as small as possible trying his best to melt away invisibly into the floor. He pushed himself as close to the doorjamb as he could and waited for an elephant to appear. The thunder stopped with a crash, and Tom heard a huge voice bellowing, singing so loudly that it sent an echo all around the stone walls. . . .

"Fee-Fi-Fo-Fum!
I smell the blood of an Englishman.
Be he alive or be he dead,
I'll grind his bones to make my bread!"

The loud song was followed by a huge roar of laughter. Then the crashing down of what sounded like an enormous fist. Peering through the gap, Tom saw knives, forks, eggcups, and plates jump up and spin in the air before landing back on the table. He could see part of an enormous hulking figure. A leg in tattered breeches, an arm in torn and patched leather.

It was a giant.

Tom hardly dared to breathe, his eyes fixed on the great shambling figure, with his cross-gartered legs.

"I'll grind his bones . . ."

Tom had never seen a giant before. He was terrified. He had never seen anyone or anything so big, ever.

". . . to make my bread."

A fast knocking came on the front door close behind Tom. He ducked into a hole in the baseboard, feeling like a rat in a trap. The huge door was opened.

"Well, well, well," boomed the giant. "So there you are at last."

The giant and the man in black walked past Tom into the room with the huge furniture. After a while Tom crept forward as quietly as he could and peeped through the half-open door.

The man in black was standing on the huge table and the giant sat on one of his own huge chairs, his elbows resting on the table. The two heads were more or less level.

"Are they still safe?" the man in black asked, in his cold, cold voice.

"Of course, sir," boomed the giant. The man in black's hair blew around his head with the blast of windy breath that erupted with the giant's voice.

"Something unforeseen has happened," said the man in black with controlled fury. "There is another

Trueheart and he is in the castle somewhere."

The giant blundered to his feet, scattering the cups and plates. "Where?" he bellowed. "Let me at him, bring him to me. I'll grind his bones."

"Settle down, settle down," said the man in black. "He's only a boy, he's nothing to worry about, he's no threat."

Then the man in black laughed and laughed. It was an unearthly, horrible sound, the nastiest laugh Tom had ever heard. Tom was furious now. He forgot his fear. He also forgot his sense; he stood up, and swept into the room, pulling the heavy door after him with a shuddering bang. He found himself suddenly exposed in a bright light on the stone floor between the giant and the man in black.

"Well, well, well," said the man in black. "Speak of the devil, and here he comes, the boy Trueheart himself."

A pair of huge hairy hands grabbed Tom around the waist just as he was about to run. He was hauled into the air and then set down inside the wooden cage on the table. The giant fastened the door of the cage with a huge knot of thick rope and Tom stood in the middle, staring out at the man in black and the awful giant.

"Let me introduce you," said the man in black. "As promised, this wee lad is the last of the Truehearts." The face of the man in black cracked across the middle into a nasty smile that showed all his yellow teeth.

"So that's him," boomed the giant. "He's a skimpy liddle boy, ain't he?"

"Oh yes, we have nothing to fear from him. I mean, look at him: he's no adventurer. No, he's just a very frightened little boy," said the man in black. "A frightened little boy who wants his mummy," and the man in black made a mocking boo-hoo crying noise. "Remind me again," he said, "what variant of that tired old name of 'Jack' do you travel under, my small boy?"

Tom said nothing and just stared back.

"Your name, is it Jacqueline, or Jacinda, or even Jane?"

The giant laughed loudly at this, amused.

Tom stood and rattled the wooden bars of his

cage in a fury. "No," he said with pride and defiance. "My name is Thomas Trueheart of the adventuring Truehearts. I'm here on the orders of the Master of the Story Bureau to rescue my brothers." Then he went and sat in the far corner of the cage and buried his face in his arms. It was upsetting to think that this horrible creature had perhaps killed all of Tom's older brothers, and that Tom himself was next.

The giant suddenly stretched out his huge arms and yawned with a great roar. "Oooohhhaahh, my, my, I'm tired now and must catch my forty winks. Would you mind keeping guard on the boy for now?"

"It will be a pleasure," said Ormestone.

The giant stood up and stamped off on his great thundering feet. Within a minute the rhythmic rumble of the giant's snores could be heard as they echoed off the stone walls.

Everything about Tom's story, all the tests of Tom's courage, had led up to this one final trap. The man in black strolled casually over the tabletop with his hands in his pockets and peered at Tom through the bars of the cage.

"So," he said, "you are an adventurer now, are you? A brave man of action, on a mission just like all your pompous brothers and your pathetic father before you?"

Here the man in black grabbed hold of the cage bars. His knuckles whitened as he gripped the wood hard.

"Such brave bumptious brothers, who go on and get all the credit for finishing *my* stories. I will be finishing this story myself, and all future stories will be finished by me. There will be no further need for so-called adventurers of any kind," he hissed. "Why do you think I elaborated all of this plot, to get your brothers to this particular place? Why did I bring them to a giant's castle, of all things? Because of your father. Remind me, my boy, what was your father known as ever since his first great adventure—it was 'Jack the Giant Killer,' was it not? Do you have any idea who invented the race of giants? You see, young Trueheart, I invented giants way back. Your father, the noble Jack Trueheart, killed my favorite creation, my first giant, older brother to that fierce sleeping creature upstairs."

Tom stood quite still calmly listening to the man, with no expression on his face. He had felt the cold metal handle of Joe's sword, untouched and safe, completely hidden on his belt under the folds of his winter cloak. The door of the cage was crudely fastened and knotted shut with a simple hank of rope. It was thick rope, but it was still only rope.

Tom felt the excitement rise inside him. He had to bite his lip to keep from smiling or bursting out laughing.

First, Tom bowed to the man in black. Then he drew the sword from the scabbard and out from under his cloak in one swift practiced movement. He held the sword out in front of him as he had so often done with his toy sword at home. The real blade split the air between the man and himself with a line of bright reflective silver. The dwarf-made blade quivered and rang with a sustained note, like a bell. The man in black was momentarily shocked into silence. Tom took a step forward across the floor of the cage and touched the tip of the sword blade very delicately against the giant's thickly tied and knotted rope. Tom smiled at the man in black and raised the sword again and lined it up with his nose. He closed his eyes and said out loud the family motto, "With a True Heart," then he brought the blade down in one swift flash against the knotted rope lock. The knot split. The taut strands sprang free, spun into the air in an explosion of coiled string and cut fragments, and the cage door swung open.

The man in black stepped back in temper and fear. He was bewildered. Tom's strength, his sudden reaction, had shocked him. "You can't do that!" he shouted.

"Too late," said Tom. "I just did."

Tom pushed out of the cage door with the sword in his hand. Ormestone lunged at him, furious, his face full of hate. He grabbed Tom's free arm and swung him around.

"Not so fast," he said in his icy cold voice. "Where do you think you are going?"

"To carry out my task," said Tom, and he looped a trailing rope around one of Ormestone's legs and pulled hard. Ormestone lost his balance and fell against the wooden cage. His skinny legs tangled in the slats of wood, but even as he tried to struggle to his feet, Ormestone pulled a big white handkerchief out of his pocket. He managed to pull himself up onto his knees, still gripping Tom's arm. He thrust the cloth out toward Tom. Tom pushed it back at him. The cloth had a sickly sweet smell.

Tom fell against the man in black, and his dwarf sword fell to the ground with a ringing clatter. Then they rolled about, tangled up together very near the edge of the huge table while Ormestone kept trying to thrust the sickly cloth at Tom's face. Ormestone's free arm was caught up in the slats of the cage, and as he tried to pull it out, Tom managed to force the bone white hand holding the cloth farther back under Ormestone's own nose.

"Sniff it yourself," Tom shouted and Ormestone

suddenly loosened his grip on Tom's arm. He fell back against the cage with a cold sinister sigh and appeared to be suddenly asleep—or even dead.

Tom dropped a length of rope from the table to the floor and turned to the slumped figure all crumpled like a skinny doll against the cage. "I'll be back to deal with you after I have rescued my brothers."

Then Tom rappeled fast down the rope from the tabletop to the ground. He picked up the sword and ran up the short staircase to the giant's chamber, which was furnished with a huge and primitive four-poster bed. All four posts were made of simple lopped tree trunks. Apart from the bed and the noisily sleeping giant, there was also another wooden cage propped up on the bedside table. A very large and forlorn-looking white goose sat sadly slumped in the middle of it. Next to the cage was a heavy iron key ring with several huge keys on it. Tom tiptoed across the room very quietly and fearfully toward the bedside table. He thought that the least he could do would be to free that poor goose, who, after all, was likely to be the giant's next teatime treat. The goose saw him coming and stood up in the cage, bumping her head.

"Shhh," said the goose very quietly, "not a sound, or you'll wake him up; he's a very light sleeper."

Tom climbed up the rough leg of the table and got as close to the cage and the goose as he could.

"I thought I ought to try to rescue you; I'm an adventurer," Tom whispered quietly.

"That's very kind of you," said the goose, "but he'll never let me go, never."

"He's asleep. I can cut you out of there in a trice

and by the time he wakes up you'll be far away."

"I'm an enchanted goose," said the bird.

"I'm sure you are," said Tom.

"No, I mean I'm really, really, special," whispered the goose.

"Because you can talk?" Tom whispered as quietly as he could.

"No no," said the goose, "something else—just look in all those eggcups."

There was a series of mysterious lumpy wooden things scattered in the shadows. They turned out to be dozens of huge eggcups. Tom went over to the nearest one. The egg inside it appeared to be made of metal, and was gold colored.

"There you are," said the goose. "I lay *solid gold* eggs. I am the Goose that Laid the Golden Egg. I suffered an enchantment and now he can't get enough of me, or *from* me."

The eggcups were everywhere, hidden behind furniture and piled under the bed; hundreds of solid gold eggs. A whole fortune was just sitting around being hoarded and wasted in the miserly giant's dark and dingy chamber. That poor goose, she would be so very useful anywhere but here, thought Tom. He went back to the cage.

"You really *are* special," he whispered.

"Thank you," said the goose.

"I will rescue you," said Tom.

"What about the others?" said the goose.

"The others?" said Tom.

"Yes, the others. There are lots more just like you, down in the dungeons," said the goose.

CHAPTER 36

The Rescue

It took Jollity the crow a long time to peck his way through the mesh of the strawberry netting and he was worried about what might have happened to Tom. Once up above the field he scanned the road all the way to the huge sinister castle. It will surely end there, he thought and flew on toward it.

He flew in through a broken upper window in the tower. A stone staircase spiraled away from him down into the gloom following the curved wall. The crow flew silently down, gliding all the way into the gradual deep dark, and soon reached the dungeons. A dark corridor stretched away in front of him with thin streams of light filtering down from rows of rusted iron grilles set into the ceiling. There were a dozen huge oak and metal-studded doors lined up on one side of the corridor. The crow looked through their narrow barred openings and through each grille he saw a prisoner. He counted the men sitting in the dark; there were six in all. The rest of the cells were empty. Jollity the crow thought it was time to go and find Tom.

Tom pulled Rapunzel's scissors out of his travel satchel. He wanted to be very quiet; the sword would be quick but noisy and the man in black might soon be up the stairs and calling out. Tom took his time and snipped away at the rope lock with the delicate gold scissors and within a minute the cage was open. The crow arrived as Tom was snipping through the ropes.

"There you are, Crow, at last," said Tom. "Thank goodness. I thought you were lost."

"Not lost, Tom, no, just caught up for a while," said the crow.

"I should introduce you two. . . ." Tom began.

"No time," said the crow, "we must fly. Come with me down to the dungeons, no more questions."

"Keys," said the goose, and as she left her cage, she picked up the big bunch of keys in her beak. The keys rattled against the bars of the cage as Tom climbed onto her back. The giant stirred. Then the crow, and Tom on the back of the goose, flew out of the chamber together and on down the deep dark staircase.

The giant suddenly shot up, very wide awake. He had heard something. He looked over at his bedside table. The wooden cage was empty; the door hung open. His favorite, the goose that laid the golden eggs, was gone. He stood up and blundered his way across the room.

"Goosey, Goosey," he bellowed at the top of his considerably loud voice.

Tom and the two birds landed in the dungeon corridor. Tom took the huge iron key ring over to the first door. The lock was just too high for him to reach so he slid the keys under the door as far as he could. He called out in his loudest voice, "Here are the keys, whoever you are in there. See if one fits. I'm Tom Trueheart and I'm here to rescue you."

There was a muffled cry from behind the dungeon door. "Tom? Our Tom? No, it can't be; this is some foul trick by that swine, isn't it?"

"No," shouted Tom, "it really is me."

"My goodness, Tom, how did you ever manage to find us?"

Tom heard the scrape and ring of metal across stone as the keys were picked up. The crow went from door to door, from grille to grille, alerting whoever was in there to be ready to leave. Tom heard grunting from behind the first door, and clickings and scrapings as each key was tried in the lock. There was a great chorus of muffled voices now from the other cells as the prisoners realized finally that something really was up.

There was a shout from the cell in front of Tom, and the door creaked open. A man stepped out of the darkness. A tall man, broad-shouldered and heroic, and as soon as he stepped into the corridor and the overhead light hit him, Tom saw that it was his big brother Jacques.

"Jacques," said Tom.

"Tom," said Jacques in complete disbelief. "It really is you. I can't believe it. My word, have I got a story to tell you."

"No time, no time," said the crow. "Quickly now, you must free the others, and for goodness' sake, hurry."

Jacques worked fast sorting the keys, and one by one Tom's big brothers were released from their dungeon cells. They stood together blinking in the half light of the corridor: Jacques, Jackie, Jacquot, Jake, and Jack, and with them a scowling dwarf with a beard.

"Everyone, this is Joe," said Jacques. "Joe, these are my brothers." Joe was welcomed into the Trueheart clan with a great cheer.

"Come on," said the crow, "we must go right now. It won't take that giant long to realize what's up."

"Wait," said Tom. "Where's Jackson, where did he get to?"

"He was under a spell, remember," said Jack. "Standard enchantment; he was going to be turned into a frog."

There was a collective intake of breath at the thought of poor Jackson stuck as a frog, somewhere, perhaps in a puddle, all on his own.

They crowded into the cells one after the other just to make sure. They were all very dark and gloomy and very empty. Tom called out, "Jackson, are you in there? Come on out, it's me, your brother Tom. The doors are open, we're ready to escape right now. Come on."

There was no sign of him anywhere; it was clear now that poor Jackson the frog was lost.

"The crow and I have come a long way to save you. You are needed badly. All of your stories are stuck where you left them and need to be finished properly before that man in black gets there and does it first and gets it all wrong. All those lovely princesses and maidens of yours need rescuing.

It's up to you all to finish what was started. We must go now, right away, before the giant catches us. You will need to climb down a very dangerous beanstalk to get back, because—you may not know this—we are in a new land up in the sky, high above the clouds."

CHAPTER 37

The Pursuit

"*F*EE-FI-FO-FUM . . .*" From above them the sound of the giant was coming, *thump, thump, thump*, down the stone stairs.

> "*I smell the blood of an Englishman.*
> *Be he alive, or be he dead,*
> *I'll grind his bones to make my bread!*"

The giant marched down the steps in a fury. He would find his goose and then all would suffer. He thought of his nasty prisoners far below, in the darkness, trapped behind those heavy doors, locked nice and tight in their cells just waiting for a grinding. He reached the bottom of the steps and lumbered over to the first door and peered in. It was all surprisingly quiet. The prisoners were usually shouting at one another or cursing Ormestone, or trying to dig tunnels with spoons. He bent low and peered through the grille on the door—the cell appeared to be empty.

"Eh?" he said. He looked into the next cell. It also seemed empty, and so did the next, and the next, and so on, until it was clear, even to the very slow-witted giant, that his prisoners might have actually escaped. Those horrible Truehearts, and worst of all, with them, his precious golden egg–laying goose.

"Grind bones," he roared, "alive or dead . . . make bread."

The giant was now in a huge bellowing rage. He went up and down the dungeon corridor. Up and down, back and forth. He looked into the empty cells, over and over, and every time he looked they were still empty. He was stuck in a bad-tempered dither and while he raged and dithered, the Truehearts made their way quickly toward the outside.

The crow had discovered another door that led out from the cellar but the giant would soon be close behind them, cursing and blundering, to be sure, and the trouble was that he could cover more ground more quickly than they could.

Jacques was all for turning and fighting him as a group; so was Jackie, and Jacquot, and Jake. "No," said Jack breathlessly. "No, no, wait, hold on, please. First, we have no weapons, remember? Second, I am sure this one was meant to be *my* story and *I* must finish it on my own. After all I hardly got to start it. We must all finish the stories we are meant to finish. I am owed a conclusion, if nothing else."

"Your weapons are here," called the crow. Sure enough, the shields and axes and swords of the Truehearts were piled in a dingy corner. They were hastily grabbed up and girded on.

"Well done, Mr. Crow," said Jack.

Then they heard a faint sound from their feet. "*Riddip,* help." It was a bright green frog locked in a little cage.

"Jackson," said Jack, "is that you?"

"Who do you think?" said the frog crossly. "Now come on, get me out of here."

"It is him," said Jack. "Maybe we should leave him in there; do him good."

"Open this thing up and let's go, *riddip,*" said Jackson.

Jacques stepped forward with the keys. There was just one tiny key among all the bigger ones on the ring. He opened the little cage, pulled Jackson up and out, and stuffed the protesting frog into his travel bag.

"Watch out, then, Jackson," he said. "Hold tight, we're off."

So they ran on, headlong, until they reached the outer door. Jacques handed Jacquot the keys and he tried each one in turn, fumbling in the darkness to fit each key and try it, while somewhere behind they heard the giant shouting. The giant had reached the short passageway, and

Jacques shouted out, "Hurry, for pity's sake." Jacquot at last turned a key that worked, and the huge door swung open. The Truehearts, Joe, Jollity the crow, and the giant goose all tumbled out and fled for the road, running back through the rain toward the top of the beanstalk.

The giant emerged blinking into the harsh light of the storm. All his Trueheart family prisoners and his precious goose were running away. This was not what had been promised him by the villainous Ormestone, with his smooth persuasive tongue. The giant stood for a moment on the step and roared at the top of his voice. "*Fee-Fi-Fo-Fum* . . . Grind his bones . . . Grind his bones," he shouted over and over. Finally he girded himself up, set his huge long legs to pounding, and ran fast down the twisty road to the beanstalk. He leaped over the rounded hills while the thunder and lightning of the storm washed and crackled all over his huge body.

Tom pointed out the top of the beanstalk through the rain. "There it is, the beanstalk; that's the way back. Go on," he shouted. "You must all climb down, but be very careful, whatever you do, and *don't* look down." One by one, all the brothers except Tom and Jack, followed by Jollity the crow and the goose, with little Joe on its back, started down the beanstalk. Tom had a promise to keep. He turned and ran as fast as he could back to the castle.

Jack meanwhile stood alone, like a prince for once, not a peasant, and waited in the storm. He was ready for the giant to come thundering around the last bend in the road.

Tom soon found Brother Ormestone. He was in the corridor of the castle, and he was cursing under his breath. He was dragging a huge sack of golden eggs behind him toward the doorway. Tom let Ormestone get as far as the first step before he showed himself. He held his sword out in front of him, and barred the way out.

"Ah," said Brother Ormestone, "I see, you have returned. I congratulate you. You will be a witness to my final triumph."

"Just stay very still," said Tom fiercely, "and very quiet."

Brother Ormestone stood rigidly where he was, his hands down at his sides, the sack bulging with gold at his feet.

"Stealing now, as well as everything else," said Tom.

"I'm not stealing, you fool, all of this is mine, mine, every bit of it. All sprite gold is mine; it was my idea in the first place. Who do you think allowed all this to happen; who created that goose? Me, of course. All this started here inside my head, right in here. I'm not going back down there. I have other plans, other arrangements. Now, if you'll just excuse me."

Brother Ormestone grabbed up the sack as Tom lunged at him with his sword. Ormestone laughed, dodged the blow, and then stood right near the very edge of the high step. "I'm not going back to that Bureau, whatever else happens," he said, "that much is certain. I have so many other plans. Oh, and I shall be sure to give my very best wishes to your dear father."

He laughed a horrible shrieking laugh, then he simply turned and jumped off the step. Tom, in a sudden blind fury, rushed to the edge. He was just in time to see Ormestone land on the next step down, the eggs clanking and jangling, then the next and then the next, with surprising speed and agility. For a moment Tom had been too stunned by the mention of his father to follow him.

This awful, horrible person knew something about his missing father. He watched, still stuck to the spot, as Ormestone reached the bottom of the steps and set off with flickering speed. Tom suspected that Ormestone had acquired some use of sorcery from somewhere. He moved so fast, as if there were some trace of sprite about him.

With that Tom came to as if out of a trance. He put his sword back into the scabbard and jumped recklessly down the huge steps. By the time Tom reached the path, Ormestone was running back in the direction of the beanstalk. Then Tom noticed that Ormestone had suddenly turned off the main pathway and ducked under the trees. He was making for one of the nearby rounded candy-colored hills. Tom had no choice but to follow him as fast as he could into the shadows, and under the trees.

CHAPTER 38

Down to Earth

Jack didn't have too long to wait for the giant. He soon thundered around the corner and skidded to a wet halt in surprise in front of Jack.

"Ugh," said the giant, shaking his hairy head free of rainwater. "Where's my Goosey?"

Jack opened his mouth to speak but then simply turned and ran, as fast as he could, his adventurer's cloak billowing out behind him. The giant took a second to realize what had happened, then he too pounded down the path, following Jack and roaring with anger. Jack reached the top of the beanstalk and raised his short sword. He lined the blade against his nose and just as the giant pounded into view Jack lunged forward and slashed hard at the giant's leg. He didn't wait to see the effect of his blow. He turned and started down the beanstalk as fast as he could.

Jack had judged his sword stroke exactly. The sharp blade cut through one of the cross-garters that twisted round the giant's huge legs. As he started down the perilous beanstalk, the slashed cross-garters began to slowly unravel from around his leg. The giant planted his big feet as best he could on the wet and slippery leaves, but losing concentration, he caught his feet suddenly in the trailing lengths of garter and lost his balance completely. He clutched onto the trunk to steady himself, while his feet slid out from under him and his legs dangled for a second in the wet air.

Jack wasted no time, and tore as fast as he could down the stalk, dashing and slipping against the leaves, lower and lower, faster and faster. He could see his brothers and the big white goose below him, much lower down the stem. The giant regained his balance and headed in a fury straight for Jack. He bellowed *"Fee-Fi-Fo-Fum"* in his terrible rage. Jack had to make sure he reached the base of the beanstalk first.

Jack dashed down the last of the leaves and reached the bottom of the stalk. He practically fell the last few feet, all the way back into the disagreeable woman's garden. Most of his brothers, Jollity the crow, and little Joe stood in a dazed huddle around the big white goose. The shrill woman shouted at them from her doorway.

"Oi, you lot, mind my garden, dropping down here like that off that great weed, whatever next?"

"Fetch me an axe, quickly," Jack shouted. Perhaps it was the tone of urgency in his voice, or perhaps it was the roars of the fast-approaching giant, that sent her so quickly into, and then so quickly out of, her house. No matter, she handed the axe to Jack and he set to with a will and slashed hard at the trunk of the beanstalk, and very soon the big twisted stalks began to lean, and sway, and wobble.

When it hung in the air by only the thinnest part of the stem, with the giant roaring, "*Goosey, Goosey,*" forty feet above them, Jack lined the tip of the axe against the last stalk, then raised it high with his eyes closed, and called out loudly, "With a True Heart," and sliced straight through the remaining section of beanstalk.

The great structure fell. The leaves fluttered and shimmered as they twisted in the sunlight, and the great stalk creaked and thundered. The giant, seeing his fate, let go of the trunk in a panic, and tumbled, hairy head over hairy heels, until finally, with a last cry of "*Goosey!*" he hit the earth with a huge explosive force.

The ground shook like an earthquake, and several tiles fell off the roof of the tower. As the dust cleared the brothers stood for a moment looking about them, just taking in what had happened. Jack shook his head. --

"That's it, then, all done. I've actually finished my story, more or less," he said. "Sadly there was no princess to res-cue this time, though," and he shrugged his shoulders.

Where the giant had fallen there was a huge giant-shaped hole in the ground, which seemed to go on forever. Jack, the crow, and the goose walked to the edge of the hole and peered in.

"Won't be seeing him again," said Jollity the crow.

"Good," said the goose. "To think of the number of eggs I laid for that awful freak. Well, I say good riddance to bad rubbish."

"What about my garden?" said the shrill woman, "Who's going to fill in that gert hole?"

"Thank you, missis," said Jack, as he handed the woman her trusty axe. "Now, we bear you no ill will, and to show no hard feelings we shall give you this." He patted the goose on her flank, the goose squatted on the ground for a moment, let out a "honk," stood up, and there was a large, bright, golden egg. He handed it to the woman.

"That should pay for any hole filling, and for any

repairs to your house that need to be done, and it should keep you nicely fed for a very long while, too."

The shrill woman was overwhelmed with delight at the size and weight of the golden egg. "I'm sorry if I misjudged you all, I'm sure," she said, with a little curtsy.

Jack patted the huge white goose. "Plenty more where that came from," he said.

CHAPTER 39

Back Above the Clouds

Tom shivered as he followed the path that twisted among the tree trunks. He could hear Brother Ormestone blundering on ahead, crashing through the undergrowth as fast as he could go. After a while Tom emerged into a clearing right under one of the pastel-colored rounded hills. Ormestone stood some way off next to a huge wicker basket laden with ropes; it looked like several laundry baskets all rolled into one. Ormestone climbed up into the basket, and Tom ran toward him across the clearing. Ormestone ducked down inside the basket and shot up again holding two large sacks above his head. Tom paused, and Ormestone threw both sacks very feebly onto the ground, where they landed with a heavy thump.

Tom reached forward with his sword and attempted to swipe at Ormestone, who ducked just in time and popped up again with two more sacks. He dropped these over the edge of the basket with a leering triumphant smile. "You pathetic little boy. You'll never be a real adventurer like your brothers or poor old daddy. A boy needs his daddy. Oh boo-hoo, did diddums miss his daddy all those years? Just think, you'll never know what happened to him now, never, for I shall soon be gone, where you cannot follow. I bid you farewell."

The basket simply lifted itself off the ground and rose quite fast, as if by some magic force. Tom looked up and saw that the round, bright, candy-colored hill was rising as well, and just as fast. Except that this was no hill. It was all part of a huge balloon, the flying contraption, primed and pumped up with hot air. The surface skin of the balloon was exactly the same color as the hills behind it, so the balloon had simply blended in with the landscape. Another heavy sack was thrown from the basket and the balloon rose faster and higher. Tom could only watch in fury as his evil enemy began to soar away slowly upward into the clouded sky. Ormestone leaned over the basket and waved down to Tom with a smug smile on his face. "Bye-bye then," he called down. "We shall never meet again. Oh, and one more thing, your father is somewhere so very far away you will never find him, never."

Tom, blinded now with tears of hatred and anger, ran forward. He was very fast. He threw himself at the rising basket and just caught hold of one of the ropes that trailed below.

"It has been such a pleasure," Ormestone called down. "You know there is nothing quite so delightful as messing about in my special flying machine." And as he waved his final jaunty little wave, he didn't notice that Tom was no longer visible far below him on the ground.

Tom held on to the rope as tightly as he could. He swung himself back and forth and built up a momentum so that he might reach a point where he could swing himself up and into the basket. Even if he couldn't defeat Ormestone, he had to know where his father was. The whole sky had darkened now around the balloon. They were flying into the tail end of the storm.

There was thunder, low rumbles at first, and then a shat-
tering crack of bright lightning, and then the cold rain hit
his upturned face. The storm took over the whole sky. The
balloon was buffeted and tossed about in the wind among
the clouds and sheeting rain. It was moving much faster
now, so much so that Tom was forced to hold on extra
tight. He could see the beanstalk below vanishing far away
toward the ground. Tom tried to raise himself to the level
of the top of the basket; Brother Ormestone's head
appeared over the edge.

"You!" he cried in hatred and surprise. "Well, I have to
say, well done for hanging on, but it won't do you any
good. I intend to go on now in a great blaze of glory. I
will finally be both the starter and finisher of my own
story. From so high a place above the clouds, above all
you pathetic little people, I will make myself into a new
legend, a new myth. See how fast we are going. Soon you
will fall from there, you little weakling; you cannot hold
on forever. Then I shall be alone to carry out the new
beginning, the first chapter of my own story, ha-ha."

There was another sudden flash of lightning that lit Ormestone's face in its cold bright light, and his eyes, staring and mad, glowed with a bright steel blue lunacy.

"Just tell me what you have done to my father," Tom cried, his words snatched by the wind.

"*I* have done nothing at all. I just have knowledge, I have spies. I have heard things in the Dark Lands, but I will never tell you, oh no. Daddy shall stay my little secret, ha-ha."

In a way this was worse than nothing. Tom had got used to the idea while he was growing up that his father had vanished on a brave adventure. He was used to the idea, however sad, that he would never be seen, never be met, and that his father would never hold him. Now the horrible Ormestone had opened up the wound again. Had stabbed Tom to the heart and twisted the knife with his horrible taunting.

Tom was slipping, lower and lower down toward the very end of the rope. The balloon was flying high over the forest, as far as Tom could make out through the freezing sleet. He could see a great canopy of snow-covered trees and the white clouds that they rested on and banks of settled snow. There would come a point soon when he would have to risk letting go and simply trust fate to land him somewhere safe below. Somewhere soft and yielding enough for him to survive the fall.

"You've forgotten something," Tom called up.

Ormestone leaned over the edge of the basket. "What, pray, is that?"

"I have a rare piece of sprite gold," said Tom.

Ormestone hesitated; if there was one thing he loved above all else, it was sprite gold. "Really, what is it?" he said.

"Help me up and I'll show it to you," said Tom.

Ormestone was torn now between his own greed and his hatred for Tom. He was only a boy, after all. He could simply take the gold from him and then throw him out. If there was no gold, if it was a trick, then he would just throw him out anyway. "Give me your hand, then, boy."

Tom gripped Ormestone's cold bony hand. He

pulled himself up and clambered into the basket.

"Well," said Ormestone, "come on, show me, then, what is it?"

Tom crouched down and pulled out of his travel bag the golden ball that the princess had given him. He held it out toward Ormestone. A bolt of lightning flashed across the sky and the gold reflected the light. The delicacy of the ball was revealed in all its beauty. Ormestone's eyes widened. "Spun gold," he said, "oh my." He was momentarily hypnotized by the golden ball.

Tom used his free hand to pull out Joe's sharp sword. It slid from the scabbard and rang in the cold wet air and he slashed upward. He missed with the first slash, and nearly lost his grip. He closed his eyes, and felt the cold rain drenching his face. Then he hit something; there was a great bang and a sudden rushing sensation. A cry came from Ormestone. Tom had cut through the balloon skin and they were now falling fast.

"What have you done?" Ormestone cried. He lunged at Tom, but Tom dodged to the other side of the basket. Ormestone shouted at Tom to give him the ball, but Tom simply threw it out of the basket and into the air. The ball was so light, so feathery, that it hung for a moment suspended in the wind and air around the balloon. Ormestone lunged at it and tried to catch it, running from side to side in the falling basket. Tom climbed up onto the rim of the basket and Ormestone, in a fury, lunged at him and simply pushed Tom off the edge out into the cold rushing air.

CHAPTER 40

Above the Cloud Lands
Five Seconds Later

Ormestone stood tall in the basket and looked down at the falling figure of Tom, and at the golden ball that fell with him. The balloon lifted a little higher into the air after Tom had jumped free, but the effect was short-lived. Ormestone would soon plummet to the ground below. Some of his cargo would have to be thrown out. The sack of golden eggs lay at his feet. His future story fund. He had little choice. He tried to pull the neck of the sack open, but his fingers were cold and the securing rope was wet. He fumbled and cursed as the world rushed up ever faster toward him. He managed to plunge his hand into the sack, and he struggled and pulled out a single golden egg. He held it for a moment and looked at it with wonder. It was hugely heavy, solid and golden, the surface smooth, and it shone with a beautiful warm gleam among all the dark clouds and sleeting rain. What a beautiful thing he had caused to be made. He could even see a little twisted reflection of himself staring back, like a madman. He threw the egg out of the basket and then plunged his hand in and pulled out another beautiful golden egg.

"Little Jack Horner," he shouted into the wind as he threw the egg out into the air, "sat in the corner"—he pulled another egg from the sack and hurled it out—"eating his Christmas pie." Another egg was thrown. "He put in his thumb," he cried as he fumbled out another egg, "and pulled out a plum"—he pulled another egg from the wet sack and threw it out as hard as he could—"and said 'What a good boy am I.' Jack

Horner, he was one of mine," Ormestone shouted, but there was no response. No one had heard, just the wind and the fast approaching trees.

Ormestone suddenly had a thought about one of those old problems in philosophy; what was it now? Oh yes, "If a tree falls in the forest and there is no one there to hear it, does it make a sound?" Ormestone realized with a terrible jolt that it was all too late, that *he* was about to fall in the far cold forest, just like one of those imaginary trees. Why had he thought of that silly conundrum of all things? Of course, if he crashed to the ground now, in whatever great blaze of glory, there would be no one there to see it or hear it. There would be no one there to see what had happened; there would be no one there to *tell the story*. There would be no story at all, not without a proper ending. "Blast!" he shouted and shook his fist at the sky as the balloon blew on through the storm.

Tom held Jackie's winter cloak as wide as he could, his arms spread right out. It acted as a brake and he felt himself slow just enough. A patch of white cloud-land rushed up to meet him, and he hit the top of the tree line in an explosion of freezing cold ice and soft snow. Then he fell down to the cloud surface, which knocked him into unconsciousness, and he was left on a high soft feathery bank of snowy cloud at the edge of the cloud-land. He woke up later, freezing but unharmed. He set off to walk what he could see of the twisted road above the clouds, where he found a trail of big golden eggs, and at one point the delicate, spun-gold ball, which lay at intervals along the twisted path. The fresh snowfall was gradually covering them over, and one by one Tom collected them up and put them in his satchel. He reached the place where he remembered the beanstalk had been. It was no more; his brothers must have dealt with it, chopped it down perhaps.

He looked down through the gap, suddenly feeling very dizzy. The world was far below him. How was he to get down? It would be suicide even to attempt it. He needed a flying contraption or a beanstalk with big wide green leaves to balance on. There would never be another one of those. Then he suddenly remembered something. He reached into his satchel and pulled out the one little dull bean he had kept back at Tumbledown Farm. "They were magic beans, after all," Tom said to himself.

He looked up at the sky; the storm had blown itself out. A bright moon shone through some ragged scraps of cloud and Tom threw the bean so that it fell all the way down to the world below, then sat and waited for the magic to work.

CHAPTER 41

Tom's Return

He did not have long to wait. There was a distant thundering roar, and something big and green rushed up through the cold air very near him. Within a minute or so a narrow beanstalk had grown, covered in neatly spaced big broad leaves. Tom swung himself across, grabbed one of them, and climbed down the leaf steps, one after the other, all the way until he reached the solid safety of the ground and the familiar garden of Tumbledown Farm.

CHAPTER 42

The Enchanted Castle, 11 A.M.
Some Days Later

While Tom's older brothers waited at the Story Bureau, Jackie and a bruised but safe young Tom stood looking up at the enchanted castle. The last time Jackie had stood on that spot, it had been a day of mist and damp, and the leaves on the briars had dripped. Today the sun was shining in a flawless blue sky. Tom waited while Jackie ducked into the tunnel he had cut all those weeks ago. Jackie pushed the central door open and went into the gloomy courtyard. He saw the soldier snoozing under the rosebush, just as Tom had described. He hacked through the new growth around the tower door, and raced up the stairs. He crashed into the little rose-bower of a room where the bed stood, just as Tom said it would, on its dais. He crept cautiously up to the curtained bed, pulled the curtains open just a little and with great care, and then he looked down.

A girl lay asleep on top of the covers. Tom had told Jackie that the sleeping girl looked just like a rose herself, and she did. She was also the most beautiful girl he had ever seen in his life. Slender and pale, her skin the most delicate blush pink, and her hair smooth and fine. He fell hopelessly in love with her at once. He bent slowly toward her; he knew now what he must do to break the terrible sleeping enchantment. He closed his eyes and lowered his face toward hers. At the same moment the princess Aurora opened one eye just a little tiny bit and peered through her long lashes at her prince Jackie Trueheart. She must have liked what she saw (a tall, brave adventurer with chiseled good looks and broad shoulders, someone a little more suitable perhaps than that first little one who came, although she did think that Tom had been very cute), because she smiled to herself just before Jackie's lips brushed her cheek with the gentlest kiss.

Once he had kissed her, she sat up and stretched her arms above her head, then she yawned and opened her eyes. She smiled sweetly at Jackie and Jackie smiled back at her, enchanted.

"Hello," she said. "I'm so glad you came. Mind you, it's been a long time."

"Sorry. I would have rescued you ages ago," Jackie said, "but someone did their best to stop me."

At that moment the king burst excitedly into the room. "My dear darling Aurora," he cried, "you are awake, the whole palace is awake; at last the spell is broken."

It was true. Jackie could hear birdsong now and all the busy noises you would expect from a royal castle.

"Father," said Aurora, "this is the very same young adventurer who has braved all and broken that spell."

"Welcome indeed to you, young man," said the king.

Jackie bowed and said, "Sire, I was simply doing my duty as an adventurer and a Trueheart."

"You may ask for anything at all as a reward, my boy," said the king. "All of the kingdom is yours."

"I already know exactly what I would like as my reward, sire," said Jackie, "and it's not your kingdom. Instead, if I may, I would like to ask for your daughter's hand in marriage."

CHAPTER 43

The Southern Lands
A Fine Morning,
Two Days Later, 11:33 A.M.

Jake and Tom and the crow headed south, and went straightaway to the royal palace. Jake banged on the door so hard that he knocked it down completely. He charged down the pastel-colored passages until a frightened flunky dressed head to foot in pink silk tried to stop him by bowing repeatedly in front of him as he rushed along.

"Welcome back, Your Royal Highness," he blustered nervously.

"Never mind all the welcomes and the bowings and the fancy silks. Just tell me what happened to that lovely girl who wore the glass slippers after I was kidnapped from that awful ball," he barked at the hapless footman.

"Oh, sire," the footman exclaimed, "she was a fraud, and not a very grand person at all. Her fine robes suddenly turned into rags. She was under some enchantment or other, and it must have worn off. The pathetic girl gabbled something about your being kidnapped, none of us believed her, and then she disappeared into the night, and was never seen again. In any case, sire, *we* all thought the ball a triumph."

"You would," Jake said. "Luckily my brother, young Tom here, did a bit of serious detective work and rescued this from the crime scene. Show him, Tom."

Tom pulled something out from his adventurer's travel bag all safely and neatly wrapped in the Trueheart cloth.

Jake issued a royal proclamation: he personally would visit every house of every eligible girl in the whole of the southern kingdom, to search for the missing love of his life, and he had a foolproof way of discovering exactly who she was.

This caused a great stir throughout the kingdom. All the socially ambitious households readied themselves for the royal visit from the handsome Prince Charming.

In a far-off merchant's house with a solid gold porch there was an enormous flurry. The stepmother had her two miserable and very unpleasant daughters ready and waiting in the gold drawing room.

Cinderella, her stepdaughter, was kept well out of the way and very busy, cleaning, ironing, and polishing in the dingy kitchen, with as usual just her little friends the mice for company.

One afternoon, Jake, Tom, and the flunky approached the same merchant's mansion. The flunky banged on the door.

The prince and his entourage were ushered into the main drawing room. A disagreeable-looking woman stood proudly by an ugly gold sofa. The two unfortunate young women who had simpered so much over the prince at the fateful ball sat perched together, both wearing their hideous best, on the sofa. Each was smiling up at him, ready for whatever his test might be. This merchant's was the last house of all the eligible addresses. There was nowhere else that the lovely and mysterious girl could be.

The flunky produced a beautiful velvet cushion, covered over with a delicate velvet cloth in a matching color. Jake spoke quietly.

"Under this cloth rests a piece of vital evidence, retrieved by my young brother here from the crime scene of my abduction." There was a sharp intake of breath from all the women. "It is a special shoe, dropped in flight by the girl I have fallen in love with. It is a delicate shoe made of spun crystal sprite-glass."

The flunky pulled off the cloth with such a flourish that it upset the sparkling shoe and it fell off the cushion down toward the hard marble of the floor. In a flash Tom took his chance. All those lonely early morning garden practices at one-handed catching were about to be put to the test. Instinctively he dived forward and he just managed to catch the tiny glass slipper before it was shattered on the floor into a million fragments.

Neither of the two gruesome girls could fit their feet into any part of the little shoe, try as they might. Their mother suddenly produced what looked like a sharp knife and offered it to one of the girls. Jake, horrified, called out, "No!" He thought that they might be tempted to try and cut off their own toes or heels just to fit into the shoe.

"It's a shoehorn," their mother said coldly.

"Oh," said Jake, bowing politely.

"Is there nobody else?" said the flunky gravely.

"No one," said the stepmother.

The merchant father piped up then from a dim corner of the room. "Aren't we forgetting someone?" he said, as quiet as a mouse. "My little Cinderella, my own precious one."

"Why, of course I wasn't forgetting her, my darling," said the disagreeable woman. "It's just that she couldn't have been at the ball. She was here at home as busy as ever. She loves to clean things, you see, Your Highness."

"Fetch her at once," Jake said with great authority.

After a moment, the servant girl, her ragged and patched clothes covered all over in gray ash and smuts and speckles of soot, came blinking into the room. Jake knew her at once. His heart leapt; he was sure now that she was the masked girl from the ball. He knelt before her himself and took the little glass slipper very tenderly and carefully from the cushion. If Tom hadn't saved it from smashing into a million pieces, how would things have ended up? Jake slipped it in one movement over her poor, patched stockinged foot. It fit perfectly.

"Will you consent to be the wife of a bold true-hearted adventurer?" he asked, gazing into her lovely pale gray eyes.

CHAPTER 44

Some Days Later
The Frozen North, 11 A.M.

Tom, Jacques, Little Joe, and the crow traveled north back into the snow and ice. Tom had given Joe his sword back—it had, after all, helped save the day in the giant's castle. Tom was now keener than ever to have his own real adventurer's sword. They journeyed under glowering gray skies and sleeting wind, the crow spending much of his time sheltering on Tom's shoulders under his cloak hood.

They arrived along with the six other dwarfs at the glass coffin, and there was Snow White, still perfect on her pillow. There was still just the faintest blush of pink on her cheek, and her lashes were delicately frosted with ice glitter. Jacques lifted the rounded glass lid of the coffin and bent and kissed the forehead of the cold princess. She stirred on her white pillow, opened her limpid blue eyes, and smiled up at Jacques. He helped her out onto the ground, and Little Joe came forward and wrapped her in a caped fur, and then he and Jacques lifted her onto one of the little pit ponies from the diamond mine, and the procession made its way back to the little wooden house.

When Snow White was properly warm, and after a hearty supper around the fire, Jacques went down on one knee and asked for Snow White's hand in marriage. She happily agreed and all seven of the dwarfs cheered. Joe said that it was good Tom had been there to stop the others from burying her forever. Then they took up their instruments and played and danced with joy, and there was a great celebration.

CHAPTER 45

Tumbledown Farm
Three Days After That, 10:25 A.M.

Tom sat on the back of Jacquot's fine white horse, which had been found happily eating apples in a nearby orchard, still wearing all its beautiful colors. Jacquot trotted it across to the base of the tower next to Tumbledown Farm. The thin-faced woman was safely tucked away in her farmhouse, busily slicing her huge golden egg into very thin but still very valuable slices. Tom sent the crow off to keep an eye on her. All of a sudden Rapunzel popped her pretty head out of her high window.

"There you are at last. Oh, and you as well, young Tom, welcome back. Did you find a tall ladder? You've been gone a very long time."

"Ah," said Jacquot, "that ladder, yes. Tom, where is that ladder?"

"Well . . . er . . . we couldn't find one quite tall enough," said Tom hesitantly.

"Mostly short ladders, you see," said Jacquot, not daring to admit that he had forgotten all about the ladder. Rapunzel was not pleased.

"I have been putting up with this for quite a long time. I've been stuck all the way up here, and dying to see you again, my prince." She hung her head, and some of her heavy fair hair tumbled out of the little window and hung down the tower wall. Tom remembered something from before.

"Miss Rapunzel," he called out, "we might not need a ladder after all." He whispered something to Jacquot.

"Won't it hurt?"

"I don't think so," said Tom.

"You ask her then," said Jacquot.

"Miss, I've had a thought," said Tom.

"Oh yes?" Rapunzel replied sweetly.

"Yes, I was wondering how long your lovely hair is now?"

"Oh, it's very, very long, Tom."

"Would it reach all the way down here?"

"Ooh, I should think so. I'll show you."

She leaned out of the high window and pushed her hair out in front of her and it tumbled, a thick golden rope, all the way down to where Tom and Jacquot stood.

"Well, that is long," said Tom. "Does it hurt if I do this?" He pulled hard on the coiled end of Rapunzel's hair.

"Ow," she said. "Not really hurt, no; I couldn't say that."

"Then that shall be your ladder," Tom said to Jacquot.

Jacquot looked up at Rapunzel and he called out, "Hold on tight. I'm coming to rescue you, my beauty." He grabbed the beautiful clump of golden hair and began to climb up it toward the little window, his armor clanking and ringing as he climbed and swung against the stones of the tower.

With every step up, Rapunzel's cries of "Ow!" and "Ouch!" grew louder, until the crow appeared.

"Watch out," he called. "The thin-faced woman is on her way from the farmhouse."

By the time she had bustled across the yard, Jacquot was already climbing in through the high narrow window.

Rapunzel gazed at him, the pain of her pulled hair forgotten in an instant. And Jacquot gazed at her. She really was, if possible, even more beautiful close-up than he could have imagined. Her eyes were the color of a pool of bright seawater. To Rapunzel, Jacquot was, if possible, even broader and more handsome than she could have hoped. They kissed gently, and Tom had to turn his head away in embarrassment, only to come face-to-face with the thin, cross woman. He braced himself for an ear-pulling. Instead the woman just shook her head and said to Tom, "Ah well, all's well that ends well."

"Oh, mother," cried Rapunzel, "I am so happy, for we are to be married."

"You mind my vegetables, young man, with those great metal boots of yours when and if you come down," she said with the faintest hint of a smile on her face. "How's our friend the golden goose?" she asked Tom out of the side of her mouth. "Always welcome here, you know."

"Oh, I'm sure," said Tom.

Rapunzel blew a kiss to Tom. "Thank goodness you stopped me from cutting all my hair off, Tom. How else would your handsome brother have reached me?"

CHAPTER 46

The Eastern Lands
A Few Days Later, 11 A.M.

Tom and the crow set out early for the eastern lands. They had Jackson with them, carefully tucked into Tom's adventurer's satchel along with the princess's lovely golden ball. Jackson's little green head was poking out at the top as he directed them back to the Eastern Gate. They were stopped by the gatekeeper at the barrier.

"Now who have we here?" he said, scuttling out of the little lean-to hut.

"I am Tom Trueheart of the adventuring Truehearts," said Tom, "and I must travel to the palace in order to complete the story that my brother Jackson was engaged upon some weeks ago."

"Your brother, you say," said the gatekeeper. "Nice-looking lad, all decked out in green; would that be him?"

"Yes," said Tom, "it would."

"If it's his story, why isn't he here to finish it himself? The rules are very clear," said the gatekeeper.

"He is here," said Tom.

"Well, either he's invisible, or I've gone blind all of a sudden," said the gatekeeper.

"I'm down here—*riddip*—you chump," said Jackson from the flap of Tom's satchel. "I'm under a—*riddip*—spell of enchantment. Surely you remember that?"

The startled gatekeeper peered closely at the source of the noise. "My, my, so you are," he said. "I suppose you'll be wanting to get changed back. Well, I've seen no sprites around here for a very long while, I am afraid."

"Never mind—*riddip*—that," said Jackson. "Just raise the barrier and we'll manage the rest."

They traveled through all the fog and mist of the east, past crooked houses and creepy scarecrows, until they found the palace with the pretty garden.

"This is the place," said Jackson.

Tom, with the crow sitting happily on his shoulder, marched straight up to the front door and gave the knocker a great bang. A footman answered the door with a very snooty expression fixed on his face.

"Yes," he said. "How may I assist you?"

"I am Thomas Trueheart, boy adventurer," said Tom. "I have come to see the king and his daughter the princess."

"On what business, may I inquire?" said the footman, wrinkling his nose in disgust at the sudden sight of a large black crow and a slimy green frog both staring at him. One was sitting on Tom's shoulder and one was poking his slimy head through the flap of Tom's travel bag.

"On—*riddip*—private business," said the frog.

"I don't think that is quite a good enough reason," said the footman.

"I think it will be," said Tom, emboldened. "I have a personal letter from the Master of the Story Bureau himself allowing me access to everything and anyone, even a king."

The footman blocked the entrance with his arms stretched wide. "I don't know anything about that. It's my job to protect the king and the princess. We had some trouble here before that upset our princess a great deal," he said.

"That was—*riddip*—because of me," said Jackson. "That's why we're here."

Just then the king himself appeared. He was wearing his crown and robes but had a pair of comfy slippers on his feet.

"Now, now, what's all the fuss and commotion, Brathwaite? Who are these people?" And the king stepped forward and peered closely at Tom.

"Ah—*riddip*—good morning, your—*riddip*— majesty; it's me," said Jackson.

"Goodness me," said the king, "how remarkable. You

sound just like a frog I once knew and you managed to say it without moving your lips at all, young man."

"It was—*riddip*—me, your majesty, remember, the frog?"

It was then that the king noticed Jackson, with his head poking out of Tom's bag. "Oh it is you," he said. "Thank goodness. My daughter has been so miserable since you upped and left. We had quite given up on you. How are you? My daughter has been rather pining for you. Can't think why."

"I've come to see her especially," said Jackson.

"Well, you'd better all follow me, then. Let them pass, Brathwaite, there's a good fellow."

They found the princess in her chamber. She stood suddenly as Tom and the king burst in on her. She had been hard at work on a tapestry, a picture of a frog wearing a crown like the king's and sitting happily on a lily pad.

She smiled at Tom, and Tom said, "Well, I promised I would bring your ball back and here it is." He fished into his satchel and brought out the beautiful ball.

"Oh thank you," said the princess, with not much enthusiasm.

"I also brought this back for you as well, just as I promised," said Tom with a flourish.

"Hello—*riddip*—princess," said Jackson, hopping out of the bag and over to the feet of his beloved in a great leggy leap.

"Oh, is it really you? Goodness, I was so worried about you after you disappeared."

She scooped Jackson up from the floor and without hesitation planted a great big kiss on his little green head.

There was a flash of blue-white magnesium light and the room seemed to spin around. There was a sudden noise, like wind tearing through trees in a huge storm, followed by silence, and there stood Jackson in all his green-clothed splendor. The spell was broken, the enchantment was ended; he was back to his old handsome self.

The princess stepped back. "My goodness," she said, "what a fine handsome lad."

"You have rescued me, my lovely princess, from an

enchantment and a life of catching flies on the wing with my own tongue."

"Yuck," said the king.

"Oh, it's yuck, all right, believe me," said Jackson.

"It was your sweet young brother here who stopped me searching high and low throughout the land for a man who could live up to the qualities of my delightful frog. He made me wait, and it was certainly worth it."

Jackson went down on one knee. He clasped the hand of the lovely princess and said, "My darling princess . . . er . . . I'm afraid I don't know your name," said Jackson.

"It's Zinnia," whispered the king with a wink.

"My darling Princess Zinnia," Jackson continued, "will you consent to be the wife of an adventuring prince?"

"Even if he was once a frog," muttered the king under his breath.

"Oh yes, I will," said Princess Zinnia. "For in a strange way I have missed you so much it actually hurt."

CHAPTER 47

The Next Day, at the Great Hall of the Story Bureau, 3:00 P.M.

The great hall had been filled all day to capacity with Brother scribes, and Brother puzzlers, and Brother poets, and Brother devisers, and Brother artists. Tom, who was still a little bruised but fully recovered by now from his adventure through the snows and clouds of the strange land, sat at the front among his brothers and right next to his mother.

There was a merry log fire blazing and crackling in the great fireplace, and all were now listening intently to Jack Trueheart. Jack was perching on the edge of the storyteller's throne. He had been telling his own story, that was, of course, "Jack and the Beanstalk." He had told it well. He had held his audience, and now he had almost reached the end. Of all the six stories, told one by one, by all the big brave brothers Trueheart, his was the last.

"*. . . and because he was so huge and heavy that great giant fell straight through the earth, in a huge thundering crash, and was never seen again. Jack introduced his mother to the goose that laid the golden eggs; at first she thought it a 'great ugly bird,' and told him so. Until, that is, she saw what that fine creature could do for her and Jack. She soon changed her tune when she saw the first of those golden eggs.*

"*So it was that Jack and his mother lived in peace and prosperity till the end of their days. He hadn't yet met his very own princess, but he was sure he would soon. The goose led a very happy life, too, as she only had to lay one golden egg a year.*

"*The End.*"

There was a second's silence, then prolonged applause. Jack looked up; his story was over, he had finished. His mother and his brothers all beamed smiles at him from the front row of seats. The Master called for silence by raising his arms, and eventually the hall went quiet.

"I would like to thank Jack Trueheart," said the Master, "most warmly for completing, and then sharing with us, his big adventure. His was the last of these six stories we have so happily heard today. Stories that were begun with such a malicious and venomous intent by the treacherous and now happily vanished and banished Brother Julius Ormestone. These stories have all been bravely completed by our special guests today. The whole of the Trueheart family has shown, as expected, exceptional courage, and they have, of course, thoroughly lived up to their noble name. But then we would hardly expect any less from our great adventuring family." More loud applause followed this.

"I can announce two important things that follow from the completion of these tales. The goose that lays the golden eggs, so bravely snatched from that cruel giant, will be given a safe home here with us at the Story Bureau. I am sure her gifts will prove beneficial to us all in the Land of Stories. And further, thanks to her great and golden generosity, the stories we have all just listened to will form the contents of the first of a new series of our Story Bureau books to be printed with pictures." More thunderous applause greeted this announcement.

Later, after a celebratory cup of tea, Tom's mother and his six brothers were taken back to their little house near the crossroads. They were driven in the grandest possible style in Cinderella's special gold carriage with four white horses. "This is the real one from the story, the actual one, you know, with all real gold leaf and everything," their mother said, proud as punch of her big brave sons. Tom chose to walk home through the woods with Jollity the crow.

Once back at the house all the brothers set to work preparing a belated surprise birthday party for young Tom. There would be two kinds of cake (Dundee and chocolate), and muffins and butter and honey. Jack baked the cakes, Jacques did his trademark jelly candies in shapes, Jacquot cooked lots and lots of tiny little sausages, Jake made a whole big plateful of cucumber sandwiches and cut them all into very tiny triangles, and Jackson, for some odd reason, decided to make a tapioca pudding.

Tom's mother, though, was worried about Tom. He had been through so much excitement and had suffered danger and injury, and she thought that now, after all the stories were over, and all his brothers were safe and rescued, he had seemed a bit quiet, even moody and upset. Why had he said, for instance, that he would walk home with just his friend the crow for company, rather than take the chance to travel with everyone else in Cinderella's wonderful coach?

"I'm going out for a walk," their mother suddenly announced while everybody was busy. She plonked her best warm bonnet on her head and set off, out into the cold.

It was not long before she found Tom and the crow. Tom was walking through the winter woods with the crow flying close beside him. He was swiping at the bushes and the trees, bashing branches and toppling gobbets of snow onto to the path. He caught sight of his mother and their eyes locked for just a moment, and he stopped. She gave a cheery wave and then walked toward him with her arms outstretched for a friendly hug. Tom stood still on the path, the fresh snow settling gently in large slow flakes on his untidy hair. He looked very unhappy.

Tom's mother stopped and let her arms fall to her side. She remembered how vulnerable Tom had looked on the morning of his twelfth birthday, how precious he had seemed to her with his silly wild hair and his thin neck. Something was really upsetting him. She took a step nearer.

The crow flew off and settled on a nearby branch, and then just shook his feathers.

"It isn't fair," said Tom.

"What isn't, Tom? Come on, you can tell me, your poor old mum. I knew something was up with you. Why else do you think I would come all the way out here in the cold?"

"Everyone got to tell their exciting stories at the Story Bureau," said Tom. "I didn't have my own story to tell; I didn't have a story at all."

"Is that what you think, Tom? Goodness me," said his mother shaking her head. "Who was it," she continued, "who went out and found all your big brothers? Who was it who faced up to great giants and scheming villains, eh? It was you, Tom, that's who. Who was it who climbed up a whole beanstalk right into the clouds? That was you as well. Your big brothers went up in a balloon, but you had to climb up the hard way. Without you, Tom, we might never have seen your brothers ever again. It all depended on you; without you there would have been nothing, no brothers and no stories." She reached forward and ruffled the snow out of his hair.

"I have to find my father," Tom said very quietly.

"Your poor father; whatever brought that on?" she asked.

"Ormestone knew something about where he might be. He teased me with it, but now he's gone as well."

Tom's mother's heart leapt all of a sudden. "What did he know about your poor father?" she asked, distraught.

"I don't know. He said he was far away. He mentioned the Dark Lands and that I would never find him, and he said I would never be a proper adventurer like my father or my brothers."

"When you've finished your training, maybe then you could set out to try to find your poor father," she said gently, her eyes shining.

"I will, Mum, I promise." They hugged each other, and then his mother had to dab away a tear.

The crow flew down and landed on Tom's shoulder. "Don't forget you were clever as well as brave," said the crow. "It was you who thought to take that glass slipper along with us; it was you who told Rapunzel not to cut off her long hair; it was you who used Joe's sword, and those scissors, and there were all sorts of other things as well. You did so much, Tom, and you haven't even started your training yet. Imagine what an adventurer you'll be after that. Why, you'll be the best adventurer there ever was, ever, in all the Land of Stories, and plenty clever enough to find your father."

"Really?" said Tom.

"Really," said the crow.

"Do you really think I was brave?" he said, smiling a bit for the first time in a while.

"Definitely," said his mother. "Come on, it's time we were getting back. It'll be dark soon and I know that your brothers are getting a special birthday tea ready for you, but don't tell them I told you; that can be our secret."

"Thanks, Mum," Tom said. "Sorry about . . . you know . . . earlier. Was it nice in Cinderella's coach?"

"Oh, it was lovely," said his mum. "Real gold leaf inside and out, pink velvet cushions, everything."

"Sounds awful," said Tom.

"Well, I liked it. Come on, I've got five weddings to

start worrying about in the spring and you will make a lovely page boy, all dressed in white velvet."

"Oh no I won't," said Tom.

"Oh yes you will," she said.

They all set off with the crow flying on ahead, and made their way back through the winter woods toward their cozy little house. Tom let his mother get ahead on the path, and the crow flew back and settled on his shoulder.

"Tom," said the crow.

"Yes, Jollity," said Tom.

"I will have to go away soon. I would like to stay with you for longer, but my job is sort of over, and I have things to do."

"Oh," said Tom. "All right, then." He stopped walking and bird and boy looked at each other.

"You were brave, Tom, you know; your mother was right. I said you would need courage and you did, and somehow you found it."

"We had fun as well, didn't we?"

"Yes, Tom, we certainly did," said Jollity the crow.

"Will you be gone for long?" said Tom.

"I really don't know."

"But I will see you again, won't I?"

"I hope so, Tom, I really do," said the crow.

"Only it's just . . ." Tom paused and took a gulp of cold air. "It's just . . ."

"Just what?" said the crow.

"Just that I . . . I . . ." Tom hesitated, "that I will need to be rescued from having to be a silly page boy at my brothers' weddings in the spring."

"I'll see what I can do," said the crow, and flew up onto a tree branch. Tom scooped up some snow and made a hard little snowball. The bird spoke to him.

"You'll need more than courage to hit me, Tom," said Jollity.

Tom laughed and threw the snowball. He missed, and the crow flew up with a happy squawk, circled over Tom's head a couple of times, and then called out, "Until the spring, then, young Tom, and some new adventures. For now, good-bye."

"Good-bye, Crow," Tom called back and waved as the bird lifted higher into the gray sky.

His mother shouted from farther down the path. "Come on, Tom, no dawdling. I could do with a good cozy sit by the fire and then you can tell me all about your story."

Tom ran up the path to catch up with her. The last the crow saw of him as he flew away was just the edge of a winter cloak billowing out behind him among the trees.

Back at the little house they had a huge birthday tea for Tom. They even ate all of Jackson's tapioca pudding, even though Tom said it "looked like frogspawn."

Finally his mother went upstairs and brought down a long parcel wrapped in string and blacksmith's sacking and tied up with gossamer sprite ribbon. It was his birthday present. Tom had almost forgotten about it in all the excitement and adventures.

"Here you are, Tom, happy birthday. Be careful with this, and remember, always be prepared, my son," she said.

He unwrapped the sacking. It was exactly what he had hoped for: his own real sword. "Wow," he said, his eyes shining. "Thanks, Mum."

"Remember, Tom," said Jack, "it's from all your brothers as well, and our poor dad, too, of course."

"He would be so proud if he was here," said his mother, and sniffed a little.

Tom drew the sword slowly from the scabbard. The blade was new and shone like quicksilver. When he tested the edge, it felt very sharp. He posed with the sword and he lunged at his own reflection in the glass door of the dresser. The blade was so new that it rang with a chime, like a bell, when he brushed the glass with it.

"Careful now, Tom," his mother said. "Remember it's not a toy."

"Don't worry, Mum," he said.

He sheathed it again and buckled it onto his tunic belt with the scabbard. He stood for a moment in the happy kitchen. "I'll show everyone I can do it, just you wait. I'll bring Dad back one day safe and sound, Mum, I really will."

Jollity the crow finally settled, as had been arranged, near a special old oak. He concentrated on the sounds of the forest in the gathering dusk. Owls hooted and tree branches creaked under the weight of snow. He did not have long to wait. He soon heard the light crackle of a sprite footfall. Sure enough, he saw his cousin, old Cicero Brownfield himself, coming down the path toward him. The crow shivered suddenly as the transformation ended. He stepped out of the tree shadow, shook his shoulders, and stretched out his arms and fingers. He had to admit it was good to be back, but he did feel a little odd.

"Well, well," said Cicero, "so there you are. I wonder what life was like as a crow? You can tell me all about it over a good flagon of ale around a good sprite fire. I think we can congratulate ourselves on a job well done. Excellent work indeed, especially from you, young Jollity." And he clapped Jollity on the back. "Come on, we must away. We will soon have new story letters to deliver, and many new adventures to arrange."

The sprites set off together through the woods, moving as quietly as shadows until they were swallowed up from view by the fading light. The trees were left to themselves, shivering a little in their white winter wear.

Farther north, somewhere beyond the dark forests, the rolling meadows, and the rounded hills, tucked into a far corner of the Land of Stories, was a lost and faraway dark place. Wolves howled and the wind raged. It was all sheet ice, and snow, and deep cold. The days were short now, and there was very little daylight left. It was already the darkening end of the day when a crumpled balloon and its tall wicker basket drifted finally to a crashing halt into the soft side of a snowdrift. Moments later a shivering figure, a scarecrow of a man dressed all in black, climbed out of the balloon's basket and stood knee-deep and seething with vengeance in the freezing snow.

The Land of Stories

Isle of Happy Ever After

Western Gate

Land of Dark Stories

Read an excerpt from
Ian Beck's rollicking sequel to
The Secret History of Tom Trueheart

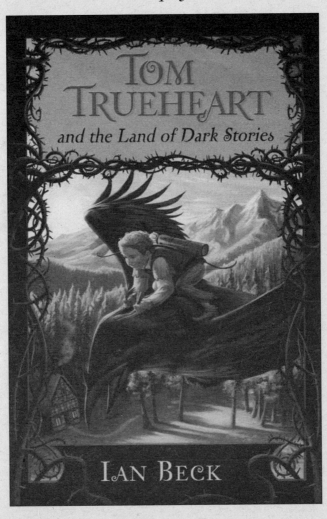

CHAPTER I

The Trueheart House
7 A.M., The Wedding Morning

The Truehearts were a family of brave adventurers, and their neat wooden house sat near a crossroads, not far from the Land of Stories. The house was painted in bright contrasting colors: red and green. The timber walls were painted red, and the shutters, with their heart-shaped cutout holes, were painted green. On the roof there were a chimney stack and an iron chimney pipe that was topped with a wind cowl and a weather vane. The weather vane was made of iron, forged in the shape of a witch riding on a broomstick with her familiar cat, a recent gift from the Master of the Story Bureau himself.

Early on a perfect midsummer morning, a big black crow landed on top of the weather vane. The bird settled itself, fluffed up its feathers, and waited. . . .

Inside the cozy house, the youngest of the family, Tom Trueheart, was already having a horrible morning. Something dreadful was due to happen to him, and Tom could not see any way of getting out of it. Should he just stay in bed for a little while longer and try to escape by staying very quiet and hiding, or should he open his bedroom window, slide down the roof, hop into the garden, shimmy over the fence, and be away on an adventure with (hopefully) his old friend Jollity the crow before anyone noticed that he had gone at all?

He would have liked to enjoy this particular daydream, but there was so much noise outside his little attic bedroom, such a crashing on the stairs, such a clattering of wood against wood, that it was hard for him even to think straight, let alone try and organize a running-away attempt. It was, of course, two of his older brothers jousting with quarterstaffs on the stairs.

The noise outside his door got steadily worse, and the moment of decision would soon come. He knew that he should get up, brace himself, and help his mother with the breakfast. He knew that he would soon have to get ready, just like all of his big beefy brothers for the

EVENT.

There was a sudden huge crash, followed by more blistering cracks of wood against wood, followed by the stomping of big feet in big boots, and then by gales of raucous laughter. Tom decided, reluctantly, glumly, that perhaps it really was time to get up and face . . . IT.

IT was the terror from the dark place. . . .

IT was the horror from beyond the woods. . . .

IT was the thing on the hanger downstairs. . . .

IT was . . . a white silk and velvet page boy suit, with a lace collar, ribbon bow, satin knee breeches, and high lace-up, kid leather boots! For today was the big day. For most of Tom's big, bold, brave, and beefy brothers, it was their wedding day!

For Tom, it was set to be utter humiliation, for he was to be the page boy, just as his mother had threatened all those months ago last winter. The wedding was meant to have taken place in the spring, but the Master had suggested waiting until the summer roses were in full bloom at the Story Bureau. And so it was: Midsummer morning and it was all about to happen.

There was another series of escalating thumps from outside his door. Putting things off for just a moment longer, Tom hopped out of bed and went to look out of the heart-shaped holes in the wooden shutters across his window.

"Please let there be a hurricane or a freak storm. Please let a rogue sprite set off a sudden blizzard of ice and snow," he said aloud to himself.

But no, when he looked out he could see that it was as perfect a summer morning as any princess bride and her bold adventurer bridegroom could wish for. Fluffy white clouds sailed across a celestial blue sky, while somewhere nearby a blackbird sang his liquid song.

"Oh no," Tom said, "it's lovely." The weather certainly wasn't going to be of any help to him today, there would be no escape.

Later, after a typically noisy and chaotic breakfast, Tom washed up the bowls at the sink. Jack sat near him on the window seat. "That's not proper work for a boy, is it? You're coddling him, our mother; he needs to keep on with some more real hard training, and soon, at that."

"Don't you mind about our Tom," said his mother, and she gave Tom a squeeze. "You sometimes do your best to make him feel small. You leave him be. Tom is doing just fine, he'll be good and ready soon enough. Don't forget, the old hermit taught him all his letters and numbers many summers ago now, and lately our Jake's been teaching him his forest craft, and he will be carrying on his adventure training with you for the rest of the summer, so there's really no need to bully him now, is there?"

After washing up the breakfast things, Tom went outside. He picked up a good-sized stick and waved it about as if it were his sword. Then he found a huge spider web glistening in the early-morning sun. He poked at the web with the stick and watched the spider as it came running down the filament. It had a fat pale body and hairy little legs. Jack always said that some spiders had poison sacs and they could give you a nasty nip if you weren't careful. Then Tom whacked a crab apple with the stick and then kicked another crab apple and chased after it across the bright grass and around to the front of the house; anything to put off the dreaded moment and THE SUIT.

Ed Beck, MB Films

Ian Beck is the creator of many picture books for children. *The Secret History of Tom Trueheart* is his first novel. He lives in England. You can visit him online at www.tomtrueheart.com.